Calvin Wes... More solid, sculpted. Almost as if he was modeled from the Greek statues at the Smithsonian.

Muscles flexed, then shifted beneath the charcoal suit coat, hinting at the controlled movement beneath.

Longing twisted deep in her belly. Refusing to be distracted, she locked her spine straight and brought her eyes back to his features.

His hazel eyes, unflinching, seared hers.

Julia broke contact first. She glanced around the apartment.

"Did you bring the file?"

"Yes." Julia reached into her suit pocket and withdrew the folded pieces of paper. "But it only explains the mission. Not what went wrong. Are you up for a trip to South America?"

"I'm the wrong person to help you."

"You're exactly the right person, actually. That's why I'm asking you to be my bodyguard."

he was lean, but not lanky.

DONNA YOUNG

BLACK OPS BODYGUARD

™ Harlequin®

TORONTO NEW YORK LONDON
AMSTERDAM PARIS SYDNEY HAMBURG
STOCKHOLM ATHENS TOKYO MILAN MADRID
PRAGUE WARSAW BUDAPEST AUCKLAND

To all of my family and my friends. Thank you for the love and
support you've given me over the past year and more. I am blessed
to have so many who care so much.

Recycling programs
for this product may
not exist in your area.

ISBN-13: 978-0-373-69577-5

BLACK OPS BODYGUARD

Copyright © 2011 by Donna Young

This edition published by arrangement with Harlequin Books S.A.

For questions and comments about the quality of this book please contact
us at Customer_eCare@Harlequin.ca.

www.Harlequin.com

Printed in U.S.A.

ABOUT THE AUTHOR

Donna Young, an incurable romantic, lives with her family in beautiful Northern California.

Books by Donna Young

Don't miss any of our special offers. Write to us at the following address for information on our newest releases.

Harlequin Reader Service
U.S.: 3010 Walden Ave., P.O. Box 1325, Buffalo, NY 14269
Canadian: P.O. Box 609, Fort Erie, Ont. L2A 5X3

CAST OF CHARACTERS

Julia Cutting—The president's personal assistant, who must choose between the man she loves and a longtime promise made to another man. The problem? Betrayed by both, she doesn't trust either.

Calvin West—A black ops agent sent to the Amazon jungle by the president of the United States. He must bring down a rogue agent and a South American drug cartel—no matter the cost. But when the cost is the woman he loves, will he be able to pay the price?

Jason Marsh—Ex-DEA agent with a vendetta, and a secret that could jeopardize national security.

Cristo Delgado—The leader of a powerful drug cartel with ambitions to rule a worldwide empire. All it will take is a few dead government agents, and his son at his side.

Argus Delgado—At twelve, he's heir to a drug empire. It runs in his blood. Or does it?

Solaris—He killed his first man at the age of seventeen. Now, decades later, killing is more or less a sport. Who are his next targets? A black ops agent and the president's personal assistant.

Chapter One

The jungle was one hell of a place to die.

Calvin West dropped to his knees in the muck and rotted vines. The storm did little to relieve the humidity, turning the air into liquid oxygen, making it difficult to breathe and his head thick and fuzzy.

A flash of lightning lit the shadows, adding a jolt of electricity to the fetid, moist surroundings.

The crack of thunder came at a snail's pace, telling Cal the worst of the storm lingered in the mountains miles away.

The bullet wound in his side throbbed. The small hole oozed blood under the muddy cocoon of clothes that stuck to his body.

He'd lost his pistol while crossing the river. The same place he'd picked up the wound.

Gunfire burst behind him. Less than a hundred meters back. Cristo's men were closing in.

"Find him!"

The order shot through the trees, making the birds flutter from their perches, their wings battling the downpour in fear of the hunters.

Cal nearly smiled over the frustration in his enemy's

command. It was Solaris. Cristo's enforcer. The mercenary was good and would make sure no one ever found Cal's body.

But, Cal was damn good himself and wouldn't give Solaris the satisfaction.

He staggered to his feet and veered back into the canal, sinking calf-deep into the rancid mire and slime beneath. Cursing the ache in his side, he trudged through the muck. Rain pelted the stagnant water, making it jump and spit in front of him, while his eyes scanned the churning current for the sleek, rolling movement of a snake or crocodile.

Bloody hell. He should have known the deal had been too easy, the lure too tempting. He should have realized his cover had been blown.

But after four years, he'd been eager to hit Delgado. Bring the drug lord to his knees.

Still, he refused to pay for his mistake with his life.

A shadow slithered along the curve of the bank. Cal swore as a boa constrictor slipped from the undergrowth and into the canal.

He stumbled from the water, fighting the riverbed's suction, his breath heavy with the exertion, his head swimming from dehydration and loss of blood.

Dizziness tilted the ground beneath his feet, while sweat and rain stung his eyes. He held no illusions. He had another hour, maybe less, before he lost consciousness. If he didn't find a path, a hollow, anything, he was a dead man.

He broke through the trees, stopped short on top of an overhang of saturated jungle rot. Quickly, he scanned the shadows.

Branches broke somewhere behind him—a brief warning before another burst of gunfire. The slap of the bullet hit his thigh, the white-hot stab of pain shot through his hip.

His leg gave out from under him, bringing him to his knees. Suddenly, the slope collapsed beneath him. Grasping at air, he hit the side of the precipice. His body tumbled over thorns and rocks and broken trees. His ribs slammed together, knocking the wind from his chest, setting his wounds on fire.

Without warning, he hit flat ground, barely missing the canal edge and the water beyond.

He struggled to rise against the swirl and pitch of his head. Acid clung to the back of his throat. Suddenly, a foot slammed into his chest, knocking him back into the mud.

"Going somewhere, West?" A laugh, thick with pleasure, rumbled above his head.

Unconsciousness slithered through him, blurring stark lines into murky shadows.

"Or are you just waiting for me to send you to hell?" The man ground his heel into Cal's wound. Pain screamed through Cal's gut.

"Haven't you heard, Solaris?" Cal struggled to get the words out before blackness engulfed him. "Hell's my playground."

Chapter Two

Winter encased Capitol Hill in a slow, deep freeze. The wind howled through the cement and steel of the parking structure, each gust strengthened by the moonless sky, the threat of snow in the air.

Calvin West slid out of his pearl-black sports coupe and scanned the rows of parked cars. Fluorescent lamps spotted the ceiling, casting the garage in an artificial glow of light and shadows. Jetlag had settled into his muscles, making his shoulder ache, his knees stiff.

Almost forty, he was getting too damn old to be chasing bad guys across seven continents.

Not that he would get any rest soon. Not with a plane to catch at Dulles in less than four hours.

With a shift of his shoulders, he fought off the fatigue, promising himself a nap during the trip to Caracas.

The shadows drew his eyes and a cold whisper of warning settled at the base of his neck. His gaze shifted over the dark corners.

Nothing.

But he didn't shrug off the unease. After thirty sleepless hours, anyone might be paranoid. But paranoia kept you alive.

He reached into his jacket and pulled his .45 automatic pistol from its shoulder holster. Slowly, he lowered the gun to his side, confident the weapon remained out of sight from the casual observer.

Heels tapped against the cement from behind him. Swearing, his finger tightened on the trigger.

"Cal."

A woman stepped from the shadows into the stark lighting. She wore a navy blue wool suit. Its jacket tailored and trimmed to hug each dip and curve of her slender form, while the skirt, cut pencil-straight to midthigh, exposed long, shapely legs. The kind that male eyes admired and female's envied.

Thick, mahogany hair was swept back and tamed into an elegant swirl that lay at the nape of her neck. The style accented the delicate, triangular shape of her face, the high classic cheekbones and the stubborn, but distinctly feminine slant to her jaw.

Professional. Sophisticated.

And sexy as hell.

The hum of awareness shifted points of contact, hitting him just south of his waist.

He reminded himself that in his line of business, sexy was a commodity, not a comfort.

"Julia." Cal thumbed the safety, then slipped the gun back into his shoulder holster. After buttoning his suit jacket, he turned fully and faced her. While her appearance was not unexpected, Cal's irritation poked at him. "The President's private secretary should know better than to sneak around in the dark."

"Sneak? Not likely," Julia Cutting responded with just enough disdain to tighten her prim little mouth. "I'm here on business."

"At midnight?" He leaned a hip against the side of his car.

The chill of the metal matched the chill in his voice. "Isn't it a bit late to be running President Mercer's errands?"

"No. Mercer never worries about working outside civilized hours. You know that as well as I do."

Cal raised an eyebrow, but said nothing. Waiting sometimes worked better than words.

It had been a year since he'd last seen her. Her eyes vivid with rage, her skin flushed from her temper when she'd slapped his face and stormed out his door.

"This would be a hell of a lot easier if it was official business," she commented dryly. "But it's not. I need your help, Cal. On a personal matter."

Julia wasn't exactly the type to need anyone, so the admission, he was sure, came at a high price.

"My help." He understood what was coming and the dangerous game he was about to play. Half truths, full deception. Take no prisoners. For the good of king and bloody country. To hell with integrity and compassion.

To hell with love.

The muscles constricted between his shoulder blades, forcing Cal to shift them under his suit jacket. "And why would you need a British attaché in the middle of the night?"

"We both know you're more than a British attaché." Julia crossed her arms. For warmth, defensiveness or plain frustration—he wasn't sure.

But the need to find out nudged him.

"I'm sure you've heard by now that Jason has disappeared." Her voice was low, her words smoothed into rounded syllables with a clipped, no-nonsense rhythm—the kind that only old money and blue-blooded, east coast schools cultivated.

But there were times, in the past, when he had stroked her soft skin and her voice hitched and sighed into a sexy, offbeat tempo that had hummed through Cal's blood—arched and bumped against his libido.

"Not unusual, considering his choice of career." Fighting back his train of thought, Cal straightened from the car and shoved his hands into his pants' pockets.

Jason Marsh had been classified as missing in action for a week. Cal found out the day before and caught the first available plane out of London.

"They told me he died in the line of duty."

"Who are they?" he asked with just enough disdain to indicate vague politeness. Not serious interest.

"Jon Mercer and Ernest Becenti."

"I'm sorry to hear about your loss, Julia. But if the President of the United States and the Drug Enforcement Agency's Chief Administrator told me someone was dead, I would tend to believe them," Cal commented, adding just enough harshness to discourage argument. "Now if that's all, I've had a long day."

The slight intake of breath, the darker flush of pink in her cheeks told him he scored a hit. Still, her feet stayed planted firmly in front of him.

"Too bad, Cal."

Stubborn woman. Silently, he swore. "Go home, Julia." Because he was tired, and understood the dangers of her involvement, his tone turned from harsh to ugly in the space of a heartbeat. "Let the government do what it does best. They'll make sure your husband's body gets a proper burial."

"Ex-husband," she corrected, her chin set, her eyes narrowed. "You're still having a problem differentiating between the two."

"Maybe," he agreed, the word silky, its edge razor sharp. "Yet, you're out here in the cold on Jason's behalf."

"I'm the only family he has," she defended. "Just because the President has given up on Jason, it doesn't mean I will."

Both President Jonathon Mercer and First Lady Shantelle Mercer considered Julia Cutting more like a surrogate daughter than as Jon's private secretary.

It was rare for a president to choose someone barely in their thirties for such a high post. Some rumors suggested a more intimate relationship existed between Mercer and the young woman, but Cal didn't believe it. He'd spent enough time mucking around with human slime to recognize integrity when he saw it. Julia Cutting wore hers like a shiny suit of armor.

While his own had tarnished many years before.

"Jason is alive, Cal."

"You sound very sure. Do you have any evidence to back up your suspicions?" He hit the button on his keys and popped open the trunk of his car. His hand hesitated over the large pink teddy bear stuffed beside his suitcase. Its white bow tie and the girly black eyes, framed with long, sewn lashes, stared back at him.

With a muttered curse, he grabbed both the bear and the suitcase.

Her eyebrow rose in a delicate sweep when she spotted the teddy bear. "Yours?"

"A present for Jordan Beck and his wife, Regina. She's pregnant. I just found out the baby is a girl," he explained, not quite understanding his sudden need to. "I've been out of the country."

Jordan Beck was one of Cal's closest friends, and at one time, an operative with Labyrinth—a black ops division of the CIA.

Jordan had recently been elected to the British Parliament, and possibly, was on the fast track to being Prime Minister of England.

If the political rumors were correct.

"You must have been out of the country for quite a while

then." When Cal glanced up at her, she shrugged, then took the bear from him. "They found out the sex a long time back. Regina's due in a month."

Car tires screeched, vibrating the steel beams and concrete of the upper parking levels.

Cal frowned; their position in the garage left them too exposed. "We'll finish this conversation in private." He grabbed his suitcase and shut the trunk. "Where's your car?"

"I took a cab here, then came up through the back stairs." When he took her elbow, she fell into step beside him. Just three inches short of six feet, her long legs kept stride easily with his. "I still have the stair key you gave me."

"Why didn't you wait for me in the apartment then? I gave you that key also."

"Actually, it's sitting at the bottom of the Potomac. Where I threw it."

Cal glanced up, but let the comment pass. "Any reason why you're using the back door?"

"Seemed to fit with the cloak-and-dagger theme you've managed to surround yourself with lately," Julia commented. "Besides, it wouldn't do for me to be seen going or coming from your apartment."

"I remember a time when it didn't bother you."

"There was a time it didn't," she responded quietly. "But things change."

"Julia," he said slowly, not liking how easily the name rolled off his tongue. Too intimate. Too many memories.

Ones that set his blood on fire and his protective mode into overdrive.

"What makes you so sure Jason isn't dead?"

"Someone left his file on my coffee table," she responded. "Inside were documented letters from President Mercer and Ernest Becenti disavowing any knowledge of Jason."

Cal stopped midstep. His hand tightened and turned her

back into him. "How in the hell did they get into your apartment?"

"You don't have to yell, I'm standing here in front of you."

"Answer the question," Cal ordered, but his voice lowered a few decibels.

"How should I know? My security system was intact." Her eyes flashed with temper. Just enough to warn him of the anger, simmering beneath the surface. "I'm not the enemy here, Cal." She tugged against his hold. "And you're hurting me."

Cal loosened his grip, but didn't release her. Not yet. Not before she was safe in his apartment. "What did the police say?"

"I didn't call them."

"Bloody hell." Cal swung open the stairway door, checked the hallway for any movement, then pulled her through after him.

"I didn't have proof. And I wasn't about to share Jason's dossier with the police."

Fear twisted his guts into a rigid knot. He'd walked away from her for this very reason.

Cain MacAlister, the current director of Labyrinth, had promised to keep Julia under surveillance. What the hell happened? "And you're sure the letters are legitimate?"

"Yes. I'm sure." This time she didn't mask her impatience. "I also understand the reason for it, but I don't have to accept their decision."

"As a government operative, Jason understood the risks that go with the job. He accepted them every time he took an assignment," Cal stated.

"Don't talk about him in the past tense, Cal. He's not dead."

They reached the lobby's elevator and she hit the call button. "The intruder left a picture with the file. He's holding an American newspaper. Yesterday's newspaper with the current headlines and the date."

"That doesn't prove anything." The elevator slid open and both of them stepped in.

"Drug cartels are not forgiving, Julia, when they find a government agent among them," Cal remarked. He jabbed the button for his floor. "A child can digitally change the face of a newspaper with the right computer program."

At least that wasn't a lie. And if his intel was correct, they were dealing with one of the most powerful drug cartel lords: Cristo Delgado.

Delgado took pleasure in what he called "public relations." Many who died by his hand, did so slowly and on camera. Later, Delgado arranged for the footage to be circulated over the internet to discourage anyone else from trying to infiltrate his business.

Cain MacAlister's people could not find any footage on Jason.

The elevator doors slid open, and they stepped out into the private entry of Cal's loft.

Julia hugged the teddy bear to her chest. Something sharp—a yearning—jabbed at her gut.

Grimly, Cal reached for his keys. "Hold on." He opened the door and stepped inside for a moment.

Julia stood in the doorway, familiar with the procedure as he turned on lights and punched in the security code on a wall keypad.

A scant minute later, he returned from checking the rooms. "Expecting company?"

"You showed up, didn't you?" Cal quipped, then took the bear and set it down with his bag. "Just making sure no one else felt the need to find me tonight."

The light gave Julia a chance to study Cal. Just over six feet, she had to tilt her head back to get a good look at his face. He had light brown hair, worn a tad longer than what was expected on the Hill. The small brown locks curled over the collar of his white dress shirt.

He was lean, but not lanky. More solid, sculpted. Almost as if he was modeled from the Greek statues at the Smithsonian.

Muscles flexed, then shifted beneath the charcoal suit coat, hinting at the controlled movement beneath.

Longing twisted deep in her belly. Refusing to be distracted, she locked her spine straight and brought her eyes back to his features.

His hazel eyes, unflinching, seared hers.

Julia broke contact first. She glanced around the apartment.

The first time Cal had brought her here, she'd expected sleek, streamlined decor and was mildly surprised at the cozy tapestry pillows, the tapered walnut coffee table and oversize chairs that flanked a sand-colored leather couch. Overstuffed and fairly new.

English country.

A touch of home, she'd thought at the time, surprised at the sentimentality from such a cynical man.

"Did you bring the file?"

"Yes." Julia reached into her suit pocket and withdrew the folded pieces of paper. "But it only explains the mission. Not what went wrong."

His eyes settled on the papers for a moment, before shifting back to her. "I need to make some tea. Would you like some?"

"Yes," she said, surprised. She'd expected him to want something sharper, like a brandy or even some wine.

"What is it?"

Annoyed, she realized if she were to pull off her plan, she needed to do a better job keeping her expression unreadable.

She lifted a casual shoulder. "British or not, I've never known you to drink tea."

"A habit I picked up recently. My jetlag demands something traditional."

She followed him to the kitchen, which was more modern in style. Black granite counters, steel appliances stood in contrast to the warmth of the living room. Fit the man more in her mind, but so did the contrast themselves.

The stuffed bear drew her gaze. Another contradiction.

Ignoring the small ache in her chest, she picked up the bear and squeezed. A soft lullaby through the thick fur of its belly.

"Cute," she murmured and turned it over, noting the Velcro seam. "I'd make sure they have extra batteries. I've got a feeling it's going to get used quite a bit."

"I'm glad you approve."

"It really is perfect, Cal," she told him sincerely. "Regina is going to love it."

"Jordan mentioned that you and she had become close over the last year."

Cal grabbed a streamlined, silver tea kettle from the stove and filled it with water.

"We did. Actually, it was your doing. The few times we joined them for dinner, Regina and I really enjoyed each other's company. After you and I split…" Julia shrugged and propped the bear up on the corner bar stool next to her. "We still manage to call each other once a week or so now that they are in London."

She settled herself on another stool at the counter. "Are you up for a trip to South America, Cal?"

"Why?" He grabbed two mugs from the cupboard and placed them by the stove.

"Jason is in South America. Alive."

"Whether he is or not, I'm the wrong person to help you."

"You're exactly the right person, actually." Julia struggled to keep her tone even. "I'm calling in Jason's favor."

Cal's eyes flickered over her. "What favor?"

"Don't play politics with me." She gave him a long, cool look. One that sent many aides scurrying from the Oval Office. "Before Jason left D.C., he told me to contact you if anything happened to him. He said you owed him a favor and that you were the only one I should trust."

"Trust to do what?" Cal questioned, swearing silently. "What are you planning, Julia?"

"To rescue him."

"Even if I owed him, I'm a diplomat from England and there is little—"

"I read your file," Julia said, taking a little pleasure in cutting him off. "You're ex-MI6. And now work for Labyrinth. Although, why you changed sides isn't stated. And neither are your Labyrinth missions."

"How in the hell did you get a hold of my file?"

"You're kidding, right?" Julia nearly smiled at that. He sounded so indignant. Good. It didn't hurt him to realize she had a few tricks of her own. "You're the one who keeps reminding me who I work for."

"My association with Labyrinth has nothing to do with Jason," Cal pointed out. "And it doesn't change the facts."

"This might." She pulled a recorder out of her pocket and placed it on the counter. "Listen." She hit the play button.

"Ms. Cutting, I'm going to get right to the point. I have your husband, Jason Marsh." The words were brisk, business-like, the tone deep with a gritty, Latin accent. "He is not dead, but he will be if you do not meet our demands. Arrange for ten million American dollars to be deposited in an offshore account of our choosing. You will be given the details once you secure the money. You will have three days to meet with me personally. Do not test us on this. If you notify your gov-

ernment of this request, we will kill him. A hotel reservation
has been made in—"

Julia pushed the stop button. "Sounds like bad guys don't
differentiate between ex-husband and husbands, either."

"He could be lying," Cal suggested. "The odds are that
Jason is already dead."

"I'm willing to go against the odds." Her chin shot up,
defiant. "Are you going to help me?"

"Possibly." When he reached for the recorder, she snatched
it away.

He sighed. "Even if you did meet them, there is no way
to call their bluff. No one has access to ten million in such
a short time. Not these days."

Julia shoved the recorder in her pocket. "I do."

Chapter Three

"If you have ten million dollars, you didn't come by it legally." Fury set Cal's shoulders into harsh, unyielding lines.

"It belongs to the government," Julia acknowledged. And Cal knew the admission cost her. "I've already transferred the money into a dormant government account. Right before I took an extended vacation."

"Tell me how you going to prison for embezzlement helps Jason?"

"No one's going to prison. I don't intend on giving Jason's kidnappers the money. The transfer can easily be considered a mistake later on. An accounting error. I'll get no more than a slap on the wrist."

"That's your plan?" Cal raged. Of course, she'd jeopardize her career for Jason. Whether she loved him or not, Jason had an inexplicable hold on Julia.

Jealousy snapped at his heels, making his next words terse. "You're traveling into Venezuela without letting anyone know your whereabouts. You plan on dealing with Cristo Delgado and his men by promising money that you aren't delivering and hope he'll just hand over your husband?"

"Ex-husband. I haven't used my married name in years—" Julia stopped, her eyes narrowing. "I never told you Jason was in Venezuela or that he was taken by Cristo Delgado's men. You haven't even looked at the file yet." She glanced back into the living room. "Or have you?"

"Who else would he be dealing with if Ernest Becenti was involved? Becenti is the DEA's administrator," Cal argued, cursing himself, not liking the fact that anger and fatigue got the best of him.

"Try again, Cal," Julia snapped. "You already knew about Jason's disappearance, didn't you?"

The teapot whistled. Forcing himself to calm down, he took the pot off the burner and poured the hot water into the cups and added tea bags. "Cain MacAlister called me. He requested that I check into the situation."

Even though Cain was technically Cal's boss, the two men shared a history that put their friendship far ahead of the working relationship.

"So Cain thinks Jason is alive."

"No," Cal replied, then settled for a half-truth. "I'm to confirm his death. Big difference."

"Yet, you flew back here from God knows where." Her brows slanted in confusion. "Why? Jason isn't here."

"I needed to get some…equipment before I take off for Caracas," Cal admitted. He placed one of the mugs in front of her. "I have no sugar."

"Doesn't matter." She dunked the tea bag into her mug. "I have excellent timing then. Delgado wants me to meet with him in Caracas."

"Where in Caracas?"

"You'll find out once we get there."

"No, Julia," Cal said grimly. "I want you to leave me the file and recorder. Then first thing in the morning, you're going to put the government money back where it belongs. I'll take care of everything else."

"I really wish I could leave this to you. I'm intelligent enough to realize that I'm way out of my league with this espionage business. But you heard them. They'll kill Jason if I don't show in Caracas."

"You're not going," Cal repeated, his voice hard, his features set.

"Yes, I am," she insisted, trying not to let him hear the fear in her voice. Whether she liked it or not, she had to go. "Please don't force me to hire someone else."

Cal reached across the counter and grabbed her arm. "You have no idea what Delgado is capable of."

"No, but you do." She glanced down at her arm, but didn't tug free this time. "And I have firsthand experience of what you are capable of."

Julia heard Cal's sharp intake of breath. But she hardened her heart, and finished her argument.

"I pulled Delgado's file, Cal. I'm hoping you'll fill in the gaps."

Cal dropped his hand from her arm and grabbed his cup, ignoring the handle. He took a long sip. "Okay, so what do you know?"

"Cristo Enrique de la Delgado. Age fifty-five. Cofounder of the Trifecta Cartel. The largest drug cartel in South America."

"That's public knowledge—"

"At one time, Delgado was one of three partners," she continued, as if she hadn't heard him. "The others being his best friends, Esteban Alvarez and Felipe Ramos. All three men were born aristocratic but relatively poor. According to Colombian social standards, at least. Rumor has it that while in their early twenties, the three men decided to break into the drug-dealing business during a horse race in which all three lost their shirts. Hence, the nickname Trifecta Cartel. With their contacts in the upper echelon of society, success was inevitable."

"Because you know his background, doesn't mean you

understand the man," Cal retorted, not realizing until too late that he'd said something similar when he betrayed her months before.

"I'm learning to," she commented, her tone stiff, telling him she remembered also.

"Ramos is now deceased," she continued. "Murdered four years ago. His yacht blown apart from plastic explosives, killing everyone onboard including his three children, his wife, top lieutenants…and his mistress. A few months later, Alvarez was shot by an unknown assailant. Godfather style, in a restaurant. Somehow, he managed to escape with a bullet in his neck. The injury caused permanent vocal damage.

"At one time, Alvarez believed Ramos's death was carried out by Delgado's enforcer, Solaris, but was never able to prove his suspicions."

Cal's eyes narrowed on the name for a brief moment. Julia would've missed the movement if she hadn't been watching him so close.

"Do you know Solaris?" she asked, going with her instincts.

"No." The word was clipped, but the jade in his eyes sharpened into glass slivers.

She didn't believe him. With a slight lift of her shoulder, she let it go. For the moment. "Since then, Alvarez and Delgado have split the business, absorbing their late partner's share and went their separate ways."

"Jon Mercer's people have been keeping them under surveillance," Cal commented. He took another swallow, this time his eyes rested on his tea, masking his thoughts. "Tell me something I don't know."

"Delgado has been married twice. His first wife, Camilla, died in a car accident just after their daughter, Alejandra, turned four."

"Yes, and some believe that Cristo killed Camilla because

a doctor told him she could no longer have children," Cal inserted.

"Alejandra is now twenty-five, graduated from Harvard Law School and just passed her New York State Bar examination." Julia paused. "She actually seems quite normal."

"Define normal."

She ignored him. "No indication or evidence that she is involved with her father or the family business."

"That's smart, not normal."

"His second wife, Rosario, is still alive," she said. "They've been married fifteen years this past November. A society girl who likes to entertain."

"And sample her husband's merchandise," Cal added dryly.

"If you follow the South American society papers," Julia agreed. "Cristo seemed to have mellowed in his second marriage. It took five years for Rosario to give birth to his son, Argus."

"She almost didn't make it. Rumors were already starting that Cristo was getting ready to replace Rosario for a younger, more fertile model when she confirmed her pregnancy."

"No information on the boy, other than he's ten," Julia explained, keeping her voice neutral.

"Cristo keeps his son under wraps. Cut off from the outside world."

"Argus means everything to his father." Fear chilled her. Julia gripped her mug with both hands but its heat did little to warm them. "Shall I go on?"

"Do you know Delgado's shipping itinerary? Who his suppliers are? Where his compounds are located? Why he takes pleasure in watching people die?"

"Do you?" she shot back.

"Your ex-husband did. And now he's dealing with the consequences."

"He's *dealing* with." She pointed a finger at him. "You're

using the present tense. You don't believe Jason is dead, either, do you?"

"I told you, I'm supposed to verify his death," Cal said, then sighed. "Even with Delgado's nasty habit of uploading his executions for public consumption, Cain hasn't been able to find any clips of Jason."

"Which only supports my theory that Jason isn't dead."

"If Jason is still alive—and that's a big if—Delgado isn't advertising it yet because he wants something more important. And apparently, he wants it from you."

"The ten million dollars."

Cal snorted. "To Delgado, ten million is pocket change. Besides, he could get the money from you without bringing you to Venezuela just by transferring the funds."

"I'm sure he'll show his hand, once I meet with him," Julia insisted.

"The hell you will. You have no experience in the field."

"I might not have experience, but I've had training."

"Basic defense training in case of a terrorist attack is not jungle warfare."

"That's why I'm asking you to be my bodyguard."

Cal's head shot up, his eyes found hers.

"That's all, Cal. You know Delgado and you owe Jason. That makes you the logical choice."

"I owe Jason, not you."

She had a debt to pay herself. "Jason told me to call in the favor if I needed to."

"It would be suicide to take you with me."

"If I die, I won't hold you responsible." Anger flushed her face, made her eyes sharp, her jaw stubborn. "You're not the only one who owes Jason, Cal."

Frustration settled in Cal's gut, a ball of fire that fed on his jealousy. He didn't want to know why she owed Jason.

Didn't want to acknowledge Jason knew Julia on a more intimate level.

"So? Are we doing this together?" She stood, bracing her hands on the counter and leaned in. "Or do I go with someone else?"

His body tightened, aware. Her scent pulsed between them. A seductive balance of lavender and the moist winter air, warmed now by the heat of her body.

Tempting fate, he breathed her in until the scent took on a power of its own. It sizzled and snapped, hunting until it found a conduit in the thick of his blood. Setting it pulsating.

Cal shifted, bucking for control. Allowing some of the frustration to break through. "All right. Just for the sake of argument, we consider the possibility of you joining me.

"If we're going to work together, we're going to have to come to an agreement." His eyes skimmed her face, rested briefly on her mouth, before trailing back to her eyes.

"What agreement?" she asked, her eyes narrowed, suspicious.

Cal let himself react, let his voice drop to a husky murmur, and let the desire burn through the twist of knots in his gut. Deftly, he stepped around the corner of the counter. Satisfied when he saw her big brown eyes widen in surprise.

"What are you doing?" She backed up until she hit the stool behind her.

It was a risk. He was moving fast.

His hand went to her hair, brushed the wisps of silk away from her cheek. Her skin warmed beneath his knuckles. Need blurred into necessity.

"I've missed you, Julia." His fingers stroked a thick lock against her neck. He felt her shudder slide over him, her silent groan slip through him.

Julia twisted her head away. "If you're trying to intimidate me—"

"A day hasn't gone by that I haven't thought about you." That, at least, was true.

"Don't you dare try to con me, West," she snapped back. But her breath caught, made her words just this side of breathless. She tried to move past him, only to have his arm block her way. "That line worked...once. A long time ago. It won't again."

"This is no line. It's a preview." He shifted forward, leaving mere inches between them. "Of what *working* together might mean."

He could take her mouth with his. Lord knows he'd wanted to, many times, since they'd slept together the year before. He'd spent hours during the longer, drawn-out meetings in the Oval Office, remembering, fantasizing. "We're going to be in tighter spaces than this if we hike through the jungle."

"What do you mean, tighter spaces?"

His hands cupped each hip, then exerted enough pressure to close the distance between them until her body fit his. "Much tighter than this."

"You can't scare me, Cal," she whispered, but her gaze dropped to his mouth. Her heart beat wildly against his chest.

"Don't bet on it. Most times I scare myself."

He heard her slight intake, saw the flutter of her lashes. Something moved in him. Something dormant that he'd thought long dead. Had wanted long dead.

He jerked away. Unable to take the last step. "Go home, Julia."

She grabbed the counter, to steady herself. *Or stop yourself from stepping toward him,* her heart mocked. "I told you—"

Her gaze dropped to his hand, saw the recorder clenched in his fist. Rage boiled, and with it the humiliation of what almost happened, what she'd almost allowed.

She clamped her emotions down between tight jaws and

ignored the tears that pricked at the back of her eyes. "Of all the low, despicable—"

"It was either that or beat it out of you." He waved the recorder in her face.

"You have no right—"

"This isn't about rights. It's about survival, damn it." Cal rewound the tape for a few seconds, then hit play. *"A hotel room will be waiting for you in..."*

When the recorder went silent, Cal's eyes snapped to hers. "What happened to the rest of the message?"

"I erased it." The satisfaction was there, taking the edge off the humiliation. But not the anger.

"Of all the stupid things to do," he bit out. "How in the hell am I supposed to help you if you aren't straight with me?"

"Do we have an agreement?"

"You have no idea what you are asking."

"I'm asking you to do the decent thing," she shot back. "For once."

He let out a hiss between his teeth.

"Someone broke into my apartment. Do you think I'm safe here? Next time they might be waiting for me," she continued, making her play.

"All I have to do is tell Cain MacAlister about the ten million. He'll lock you up."

"Go ahead." She brushed the threat aside, buried the fear deep. More than her pride was at risk. So much depended on this. "Whoever gave me Jason's file is high up in the government. Only personnel with top clearance have access to that file."

"You had access to mine."

She ignored him. "That same person could be driving this deal. They'll find out if you have me arrested. And I'll give you good odds I'll be dead within a few days. Cell or not."

The tightening of his jaw told her she'd won. Still, she

pushed a little more. "I have to be in Venezuela in less than forty-eight hours. We're wasting time bickering over this, when you have no choice but to come with me."

"This is turning out to be one hell of a payback." Cal yanked a hand through his hair. "The promise I made to Jason didn't include getting you killed."

"Then don't get me killed," Julia reasoned, crossing her arms to mask her shaking limbs.

"Bloody hell."

CAL SETTLED BACK INTO HIS SEAT, shifting slightly to accommodate the limited space of the airplane's coach section.

He insisted that he and Julia board separately, both under aliases. He'd chosen a seat toward the back. One that gave him a full view of the passengers, but far enough away from the engines so his hearing wouldn't be impaired.

The fact that he owned a Learjet—a benefit from solid family investments—didn't improve his mood. But flying privately posed more problems then he was willing to deal with.

The passenger beside him—a solid man in his fifties with a beard and smelling of garlic—snored through an open mouth, making Cal rethink what he could deal with.

His gaze scanned the section. Many families, a few couples, even one or two single mothers traveling with babies. The rest seemed to be a spattering of solo men and women. Most of the men dressed in cotton slacks and sport shirts, the women in trousers and simple tops. Business casual.

He'd worn an oxford-white shirt tucked into tailored black slacks. And because of his fake identification, an Air Marshal-approved pistol tucked into its holster at his ankle.

Business ready, he thought coldly.

Julia sat a few rows ahead. An empty seat divided her and an older woman with a fluff of white cotton for hair.

Her head rested against the window of the plane, still. Most likely asleep.

The sunlight spilled through the small, square porthole, setting dark strands of hair into a golden fire.

It had been like that the first time he'd seen her in Jon Mercer's office. Cool. Efficient. The lights catching her just right, dazzling him. Then she smiled. A full-on mischievous smile that revealed a sexy little dimple at the side of her mouth.

He rubbed his chest, trying to ease the tightness. It had been the first time in his life Cal had been sucker punched.

Uncomfortable with the memory, he shifted the gun to his pocket and unfolded himself from his seat. Within moments, a female flight attendant approached.

"Can I get you something, Marshal?" She was an attractive woman in her late twenties, with a short bob of blond curly hair, and an invitation in her baby blues.

"The lavatory?"

She gestured to the back of the plane, used the opportunity to take a lingering look. "If you need anything else, let me know."

"I will," he promised easily.

Cal reached the bathroom, closed the door, then turned the lock. He pulled out his satellite cell phone.

Quickly, he punched in the number.

"MacAlister."

"It's West."

"It's about damn time. What the hell is going on, West?" Cain nearly shouted the words. "You had specific orders. Bringing Julia Cutting on this operation wasn't part of them."

So Cain had been keeping Julia under surveillance, then. It was the only way the Labyrinth director would have known about their pairing up. "I have the situation under control. We're still a go on locating your missing equipment."

"You were supposed to notify me if Julia made contact. Why didn't you?"

"She didn't find me to work out a deal. She needed a bodyguard for her trip to Caracas."

"Don't trust her, Cal."

"Julia isn't a traitor, damn it. She's a pawn and you know it. She'd never roll over on Jon Mercer, Cain."

"All I know is that I'm missing a state-of-the-art technical component."

The DEA's new Drug Enforcement Retriever. Nickname: MONGREL.

The United States government had developed a drug detector that could find a smuggled shipment of narcotics by simply analyzing compound structure found in the air or in the residue from fingerprints and most other surfaces. The prototype could read a millionth of a gram. A particle so small that up until now could only be seen under a microscope.

It was a breakthrough in high technology that could disrupt drug shipping for months, even years until the drug cartels could counter its effectiveness.

Unless they had the prototype.

"Julia Cutting is my primary suspect," Cain insisted. "I've seen women betray their husbands, their own children for power. The President of the United States is nothing."

"She admitted to taking ten million out of the government coffers. Not to heisting the MONGREL."

"What ten million dollars?" Cain let go with a string of obscenities. "How did she do that?"

A small smile twitched across Cal's lips. Cain didn't like being outmaneuvered. Simply because that meant he wasn't an expert strategist.

"Check the government account books and find out," Cal

advised. "It's ransom money, Cain. I heard the tape Delgado sent her."

"Delgado doesn't need ten million dollars."

"I agree." Cal rubbed the back of his neck. "I haven't figured out what he really wants yet. He might suspect she has the MONGREL, but my fear is he hasn't laid the past to rest. If that's the case, she's walking into a death trap."

"You both are, so be careful," Cain warned.

"I left the recorder in the top drawer of my nightstand. Get it and have Kate analyze it. Julia erased most of the instructions. See if Kate's people can retrieve them for me. I want to know exactly what Delgado wants."

"He wants the MONGREL. And Jason Marsh supplied the means if he gave it to Julia. Roman is fit to be tied that Jason walked out of his security lab with the prototype."

Roman D'Amato was Cain's brother-in-law, and an ex-Labyrinth agent. After marrying Cain's sister, Kate, Roman created a worldwide security corporation that specialized in state-of-the-art technology.

"Roman can have him, after I'm finished with him."

"You mean if there's anything left," Cain commented wryly. "Once Delgado gets the prototype, it will circumvent any hope we have to contain his activities and bring him down."

"Whatever Delgado is after, it's not to use Julia as a hostage," Cal continued, not willing to argue Cain's point quite yet. "He obviously needs Julia to arrive in Caracas on her own, otherwise he would have had her snatched from her apartment."

"Not with the surveillance I had on her."

"Your surveillance didn't keep Delgado's men from leaving the tape recorder, Cain."

"I'll find out why," Cain promised. "Delgado must suspect Julia has the MONGREL."

"How?" Cal asked.

"Good instincts. Jason. Or tip-off from our ranks," Cain growled. "I'd bet Kate's fortune on the last."

"Not yours?" Cal smiled. Kate and Cain were siblings. Both with raven-black hair, slate-gray eyes and a hell of a Scottish temperament. And both, along with their brother, Ian, were heirs to the MacAlister Whiskey fortune.

"Hell, no," Cain grunted. "Look, I'll deal with things here. Your attention needs to be there. Once Julia Cutting finds out I've sent you over there to kill her husband, she becomes a major iiability for you."

"Ex-husband," Cal corrected with a hard edge. "Leave Jason and Julia to me, Cain. That's what you pay me for."

"You're sounding like she's got you wound up again, Cal," Cain remarked, then paused for a moment. "Julia Cutting's sudden involvement doesn't change our original operation. Don't make me regret putting you on this. Do your thinking out of bed and get the job done. Find our mole. Find Jason. But most of all, find the MONGREL."

"I will."

"You'd better," Cain ordered, his tone unbending. "Or I'll find someone who can."

Chapter Four

"Taxi, Miss?"

"Si. Gracias," Julia answered the airport skycap, her smile now more tired than triumphant.

They'd flown through the early hours of the morning, arriving midafternoon in Caracas. Lack of sleep made her eyes gritty, her head ache. Ignoring both, she adjusted her bag strap farther onto her shoulder and stepped to the curbside.

Cars honked, prodding the pedestrians into motion who ignored the green glare of the traffic lights.

"Is this your first time in Venezuela?" The skycap was an elderly man with a shock of silver hair on a round face. His black eyes seemed softer than most. Kind.

"You are alone?" The man spoke in English, rolling his R's in a lyrical manner. He glanced around her for a traveling companion.

"Yes."

"Please. You will want to take this taxi." The man waved to a small white car on the other side of the street, ignoring the row of taxis behind him. The driver next in line honked in protest, but the skycap merely turned his back on him and nodded toward the taxi making a U-turn in front of them.

"Renalto is a friend of mine and honest. He knows the city well. He will take you wherever you need to go."

Julia regarded the older man for a moment, her smile

no longer tired, but grateful. *"Gracias,"* she repeated and handed the skycap several pesos. "Much appreciated."

Renalto parked in front of her and jumped eagerly from the car. He smiled, revealing a gold tooth that flashed in the sunlight.

"Buenos días." He came around to her side and opened the back passenger door on the sedan.

"Buenos días."

"You take care of the lady, Renalto. She is here for business, not your shenanigans."

"I am always the gentleman, old man," Renalto replied, his grin wider. "Unless the ladies prefer otherwise."

"This one does not," Julia remarked, unable to curb the laughter that filtered through her words.

"I am still at your service, *señorita.*" Renalto bowed at the waist. "You see, Leopold, I can be a gentleman."

The older man shook his head even as Renalto reached for her carry-on case.

Julia stopped his hand. "I'll keep it, if that's all right."

"Of course." Instead, he waved his hand toward the passenger seat. "Welcome to Venezuela."

"Ms. Cutting?" A man approached, his black hair slicked back on his scalp, his black suit—too dark for the heat of the day—tailored to emphasize the steroid-enhanced muscles beneath, matched the dark sunglasses that covered his eyes but didn't quite cover the pock-mark scarred cheeks.

Without warning, he pulled a pistol from beneath his suit coat and clubbed Renalto on the back of his head. The driver fell into the side of the taxi then hit the pavement.

The man pointed the weapon at Julia. "Come with me."

When Leopold stepped forward, Julia instinctively blocked him with her arm. "Don't," she warned Leopold, her eyes not leaving the gunman. "And if I refuse to come with you?"

The man in the suit waved his pistol toward Renalto. "Leave him or join him. Your choice."

"We'll pass, Jorgie." Cal stepped behind the man, grabbed the gun. Before the man could react, Cal jerked the man's wrist sideways. The bone snapped, the man grunted with pain and dropped the gun. Cal rammed his elbow in the man's face, felt the cartilage give way, the blood spurt. "The lady doesn't like violence."

Cal kept the pistol and shoved the man aside. "Let's go."

"The driver," Julia warned. She knelt in front of Renalto. "He needs our help."

"I'm okay, *señorita,*" Renalto whispered, wincing. Then he reached for his head. "Go with your friend."

"I will take care of him," Leopold interjected, already reaching for Renalto's arm to help him up.

Cal opened the taxi's passenger door and shoved Julia in, then tossed his bag in after her.

"Put your seat belt on," he ordered.

After slamming her door shut, he reached into his pocket and flicked a business card on Jorgie. "Tell your boss I'll be in touch."

Without waiting for a reply, Cal slid behind the steering wheel.

"Are you all right?" Cal glanced at the rearview mirror, threw the car into gear, then pressed his foot against the gas.

"Yes," Julia answered, ignoring the tremor in her fingers and snapped the seat belt in place. "What did you give him?"

"A warning." They shot forward into traffic. Cal swore and swerved past an oncoming car. "Hold on."

"You called him Jorgie," Julia said observingly. "Is he one of Delgado's men?"

"Yes," Cal replied, then jerked the wheel to avoid a man on a bicycle. "Jorgie Perez. Although I doubt it is his real name."

"How do you know him?"

"Cain MacAlister gave me a rundown on most of Delgado's men. I recognized Jorgie from a photograph."

"When were you going to share Cain's information?" She asked the question in a quiet voice, but Cal wasn't fooled.

"You've done your research, remember?" he responded wryly. When she didn't answer, he continued, "Jorgie knew you were on that flight. He made contact too quickly otherwise."

"Our aliases came from Labyrinth, right?"

"Yes."

"So whoever had access to Jason's files also has access to Labyrinth's," Julia concluded. "That means we can't trust the good guys."

"Exactly," Cal admitted, impressed with her reasoning.

"Including Cain?" she asked quietly.

"I'm not sure yet."

"So what now?"

"We switch identities one more time. But the next one we use is from one of my private sources," Cal replied. "And we keep to ourselves for a while."

"You mean no more contact with Labyrinth."

A development that worked well with Cal for the moment. His phone call with Cain had hit too close to home.

"You've already told me my job is to keep you out of danger and to find Jason. Whatever it takes," Cal reminded her. "It would help if you told me why Delgado wants you here. It's not because of the money."

"I told you, I don't know," Julia said, uncertain. "The obvious reason would be that I work for the President and have access to top clearance files."

"If that were the case, he'd want you back in Washington where you'd be more use to him."

Cal took a hard right and headed down another main street.

Suddenly, car tires squealed behind them.

"We've got a tail."

Julia caught the dark sedan in her side mirror. "Delgado's men?"

"Probably." Cal swerved into the far right lane to avoid a motor scooter. "Hold on." He crossed two lanes of traffic and skidded into another left turn.

A screech of tires followed a blare of a car horn. Within moments, the sedan appeared and sped down the street after them. "Which hotel were you going to stay at, Julia?"

"The Gran Paraíso."

He glanced at his rearview mirror and ran through the red light. Julia grabbed the dashboard, held on as Cal swerved to miss oncoming traffic. Suddenly, he hit the brake and fish-tailed into a nearby alley.

A minute later, the black sedan rushed past.

"Delgado owns the Gran Paraíso and several others in the area," Cal remarked, his gaze on the rearview mirror.

"I know that. I'd counted on my alias." She leaned back and took a deep breath, trying to calm her heart before it burst from her chest. "You sound like you know Delgado personally."

"I've had my run-in with his people in the past," Cal said noncommittally. His gaze swept over her sleeveless cream-colored blouse and burgundy skirt. "What else did you bring to wear?"

"Not much. A pair of slacks. Some shorts. A few cotton shirts."

Julia looked up, saw Cal's eyes on her, felt her blood heat, her skin turn pink. "Why?"

"You're a beautiful woman, Julia." Cal drove the car down the alley and turned onto the next main street, heading in the opposite direction of the black sedan.

"Somehow I don't think you're complimenting me," she said wryly.

"I'm not. Men notice beautiful women, and then remember them. You can bet Delgado's men have pictures of you. I've been thinking about it since the plane trip." Mainly because every male that Julia passed took a lingering second glance, annoying Cal. "You're going to need a new image."

He parked the car on a nearby street. Cal grabbed their bags. "We're going to need to alter your appearance a bit. Something more suitable for the drug-smuggling business. We'll make a stop at a few local shops. Then I need to make some phone calls."

"Delgado must not have trusted me to follow instructions." The lie slipped over her tongue, but left a bitter taste behind.

"He's Colombian Cartel," Cal reminded her, then waved another taxi down. "He doesn't trust anyone. Not even his wife."

Rosario Conchita de la Delgado y Martínez shifted away from the body next to hers and closer to the wine glass on the nightstand.

She tipped the glass upside down, let the few drops fall to the carpet. Annoyed, she reached for the bottle nearby and poured the remaining burgundy into her glass. The buzz from her recent high had all but disappeared, forcing her to make do with alcohol.

"Isn't ten in the morning a little early for drinking, even for you?"

"Nothing is too early for me." Rosario took a long sip from the glass, not so much enjoying the bite, but needing the burn of it on her throat and in her stomach. Take the edge off the cravings until she scored more cocaine from Cristo's guest supply. "What do you care, darling?" She scooted back against the headboard and pulled a silk sheet up over her ample breasts. "It won't interfere with our little rendezvous."

Solaris glanced at the woman in the bed. Over a dozen years younger than her husband, she'd been bargained for and bought at the age of eighteen. It had taken her several years, and quite a few miscarriages before she produced the treasured male child for Cristo.

No longer able to have children, she served little purpose in her household. And held little more value than the fine china or Persian rugs.

"What are you thinking about?"

"How beautiful you are," Solaris replied smoothly. "And how much other women must envy you."

A delicate brow rose in spite of his sincerity. "And you've known many women." Still, her fingers loosened, allowing the sheet to slide a few inches toward her waist.

Despite her drug habit, her body reminded him of a nineteen fifties starlet's. The long, ebony hair that draped and curled over golden skin and satin curves. The plump, pouty lips made simply to drive men mad.

Solaris grew hard in anticipation.

Rosario's gaze drifted down to his lap. "Twice isn't good enough for you?" She let out a small, female purr. But the breathlessness was there, too, inciting both of them.

Slowly, Solaris tugged on the sheet, the whisper of it seductive as the material slid over her skin until she lay completely exposed.

"I have to be back shortly after eleven. Any later, we risk discovery."

Fear edged her words, but arrogance made her chin tilt upward. They both knew if found out, they'd die. Or worse.

He dipped his index finger into her glass, then traced one pink nipple with the red liquid.

A soft sigh slipped from her lips. Her hand slid behind

his neck, her nails scratching just enough to get his attention before tangling themselves in the hair at his nape. She leaned back against the headboard and closed her eyes.

"I think…" Smiling, he lowered his head, enjoying the feel of her fingers flexing against his scalp. "…some things in life are worth the risk."

Chapter Five

Most times I scare myself.

Cal's earlier words drifted through Julia's mind, leaving her wondering what he'd meant. Even at their worst moment together, he'd never sparked fear in her, only anger. She stifled a small shiver. That was then, this was now.

After they abandoned the car, Cal flagged down a taxi and took her shopping most of the afternoon. She'd tried on nothing, drew no attention to herself, not that it mattered.

From the moment they walked into a store, he'd taken charge. He ignored her suggestions and made his own choices.

Bold, jeweled colors, thin materials, admittedly feminine styles. But all at prices that would put her bank account in arrears for a whole year.

"Still pouting?"

"I don't pout." She never had, but if she could, today would've been the day. Instead, she straightened her shoulders and looked down her nose. A tactic that served her well in the Oval Office.

Cal laughed. "Could have fooled me."

He set their shopping bags on the floor and opened the door to a high-rise apartment.

"Stay here." He grabbed his gun from its holster and disappeared past the doorway.

"Jerk," she muttered.

"I bloody well heard you," Cal admonished from some-where in the apartment.

After sounding the all clear, he appeared at the door. "If you're going to call me names, at least do it to my face."

"Why, when I take so much pleasure in doing it behind your back?" Julia snagged the shopping bags, then slipped past him through the doorway.

"What next?" The blast of air-conditioning felt good against her skin. She set the packages on a nearby couch, lifted the hair from the nape of her neck and closed her eyes.

She wore her hair shorter now, styled into a sleek cap of sable that was parted at the side and cut into a blunt slant. It brushed against the smooth line of her jaw, drawing the eye down the delicate line of her neck.

"That depends on you." The underlying edge had her eyes open, but whatever she thought she heard was gone. He shoved the pistol into its holster behind his back, then slipped off his jacket.

"Are you going to start sharing information with me?" He loosened his tie and unbuttoned the top three buttons of his shirt, leaving the strong column of his neck and a bit of his chest visible.

"For instance?" Julia glanced away, ignoring the skip in her pulse, the desire that tickled the back of her throat.

"We can start with the bank accounts that you placed the money in."

"No." Her hand fell away, the hair settled once again on her nape. "And before you rip into me, I'm not keeping it from you out of spite, Cal. It's my insurance. I need to be part of this mission."

"Since when has this become a mission?" Cal asked wryly. "I consider it a wild goose chase."

Julia sank onto a matching love seat, then resisted the urge to slip off her leather sandals and fling one at Cal's head.

Instead, she settled for a small toss under a nearby coffee table and studied her new home.

The apartment reflected the romantic elegance of a century-old Spanish villa. Rustic reds and muted greens threaded the room, enhanced the oversize adobe fireplace and exposed-beam ceiling. Linen drapes of a pale, buttery-yellow billowed gently against the open windows and balcony doors. The scent of the warm Caribbean breeze tugged at the senses, tempting those inside to wander out, she was sure, to the sun-warmed balcony and the ocean view beyond.

"Why didn't you tell me Jason was your friend?" she asked. "We were together for nearly six months and you never mentioned it."

"Because Jason and I weren't friends," Cal answered. "We weren't anything."

"And yet, you owe him."

"I owe a lot of people many different things, Julia. And some owe me. It's the nature of my job. You've worked in politics, you've seen Jon Mercer operate. The man borders on being one of the best con artists of our time."

He crossed over to a small glass bar beside the balcony doors. "Want something?"

"No, thanks." She loved Jon like a father, so it was hard for her to be at odds with him now. Even harder to believe the worst of him.

Stubborn Irish, his wife Shantelle called him in private. With his charming ways and wicked words.

Approaching his midsixties, President Mercer defined the term "larger than life" with a set of strong, broad shoulders, an even gait to his walk and, on most occasions, an even temperament. He was quick to laughter, quicker when the joke was on him, but swift and scathing when it came to dispensing his more difficult duties.

Jon Mercer saw only the black and white when it came down to the laws. Of humanity or the land. He compromised out of necessity—for the people who entrusted him with their lives and the well-being of their children. But on a deeper, personal level, there existed no gray areas.

And Julia admitted silently, that was what she feared the most.

Restless, she stood and walked to the window. The sun sank toward the ocean, painting the beach in tangerine hues, shaping the waves until they tossed and turned with the incoming tide.

"You're like him, you know." She turned to Cal. Frustration scraped at her nerves, even while its cause evaded her. "I never really understood that until now."

"Like who?" Cal opened a cabinet underneath the bar and pulled out a bottle of whiskey.

"Jon Mercer."

Cal's lips twitched with amusement. "You'd bloody well better be joking, sweetheart. I haven't aged that much since you've last seen me."

"I'm not talking in physical likeness."

But in retrospect, she saw that, too. A younger Jon Mercer, an older Calvin West.

His shoulders flexed beneath the white dress shirt just a bit when he poured three fingers of the whiskey into a highball glass. Her eyes followed the lines, the tailored fit of the cotton from the shoulders to his chest to the flat of his stomach.

It hadn't been that long since she'd touched the warm contours beneath.

"Do you want me to step from behind the bar so you can finish the job?" Cal said softly.

Startled, Julia looked up, her breath hitched in her chest.

He stilled at the sound, letting his gaze catch hers. Something in his eyes sharpened, then turned almost predatory.

She forced herself to breathe.

"How do I remind you of Jon Mercer, Julia?"

Each of his words drifted over her, low and velvet-smooth against her skin. Small electric shocks pricked at the base of her spine even as the warning bells went off in her head.

"For king and country," she said, cursing the fact her voice broke just a little. "No middle ground. No matter what it takes. Or who it destroys," she repeated, just managing to keep the hurt from filtering through.

"It sounds a bit heroic, doesn't it?"

"If it did, that wasn't my intent," she retorted. "I was aiming more for calculated and…"

Dangerous.

He stepped from behind the bar, and her gaze dipped to the narrow hips, the lean thighs barely hidden by the tailored lines of his trousers.

And sexy as hell.

Her muscles went lax, her body trembled. Just with words and a few heated glances.

Damn him.

"And?" he challenged her, and took a swallow from his glass before he set it on the counter. The request was direct, a double-edged sword.

Images of them, naked, their limbs tangled, his body hot and hard against hers.

Julia closed her eyes against the memories.

"You're not going to get fainthearted on me, are you?" He spoke the words low, against her ear.

Her eyes flew open. He'd moved silently, quickly until he stood mere inches from her. She'd forgotten how quietly he moved. "Let's not bring my heart into this."

"Into what?" he murmured.

They were no longer talking about Jon Mercer. His finger touched her ear, traced its delicate curve.

Julia shivered. He gathered her close. His fingers drifted down her spine, making small, lazy circles over her back. She curled into him.

Before she could answer, his mouth covered hers, coaxing, caressing.

"Just one. The one I wanted at the apartment. The one I've been craving since…" He captured her groan in a long, deep kiss. Desire rolled through her, over her, in an unleashed tidal wave of heat.

Drowning, she broke away. "Stop, Cal."

Hadn't she hitched that ride? A whirlpool of molten lava that tugged at her until her senses spiraled into a thick vortex of desire and anger. Fast and furious, she'd loved every minute of it.

Loved *him*.

Until he'd played her. Used her to get information for MI6, England's answer to the CIA.

Top secret information.

Seduce the President's secretary, steal files from her computer and win the game.

She pulled back, broke contact and forced herself to look at him again. Past the dark, set, sexy features to the cold, calculating depths underneath.

"I think I'd like a drink now." She stepped away, praying her legs wouldn't buckle beneath her as she made her way to the love seat.

For support, she settled deep into the cushions. For spite, she crossed her legs, deliberately letting the material slide up mid-thigh.

"You don't mind, do you?"

His gaze wandered up from her bare feet, over her knees

to the tip of the hem. Only then did he shift back to her face. His fingers flexed for a brief second at his side.

"No." The word was clipped, its sting sharp enough to make her flinch.

Almost.

SOLARIS LEANED ON THE RAIL OF THE freighter, *The Hyperion,* and took a long drag on his cigarette. The smoke caught in his chest and held. For a moment he enjoyed the sting of the nicotine, then slowly exhaled.

The ship rolled beneath his feet. The rhythm set by a nearby crane as it settled orange and brown cargo containers onto *The Hyperion*'s deck.

He was a fisherman's son. Spent his youth hauling nets, trawling traps, setting hooks and sails. The work roped the muscles of his six-foot frame, added bulk to the wide shoulders and barreled chest, set steel in his spine.

Over the years, he'd lost his father and two brothers in the storms, while his cousins lost limbs and with them, the taste for the sea.

But Solaris continued, taking pride in what his father had passed to him. The skills, his family's name. Until the commercial fishing companies muscled in and stole their livelihood—leaving his mother and sisters to starve.

The water lapped up against the side of the ship, its spray caught in the tug of the wind leaving a sheen of salt water sparkling in the air, the taste of the ocean at the back of his throat.

At eighteen, Solaris had killed his first man. A lawyer who came to repossess their family home and business. There was no remorse, no pity. Nothing but utter satisfaction when the man took his last breath with Solaris's knife in his chest, his hand still on the hilt.

It was then he realized his other talent. And killing had become his new line of work.

For the first fifteen years, he drifted from country to country, hiring his skills out to those who could pay for them, learning his trade, building his fortune.

Then he met Cristo Delgado.

In the years he worked for Cristo, Solaris's bank account had quadrupled. He even managed a few deals on the side.

Though he had never returned home, he continued sending money to his mother and sisters through untraceable means.

A limousine pulled up near the gangway. Solaris pitched his cigarette into the water and stepped from the railing.

Cristo's lieutenant, Jorgie, got out of the front passenger seat and stood next to the limo. A bandage crossed his nose and connected two swollen black eyes. Another wrapped around his right hand and wrist.

A moment later, four additional homegrown thugs emerged from a nearby black sedan and flanked the limousine.

Once his men appeared in place, Cristo emerged from the limo, said something to Jorgie while he buttoned his Armani suit coat, and slipped on a pair of mirrored sunglasses.

Despite his age, Cristo managed to stay trim and fit. Driven by vanity, he worked out regularly in the villa's indoor pool. But besides a mistress or two, Solaris's boss had no other vices.

Cristo glanced up and smiled, revealing a row of white teeth that flashed against the tanned face and well-groomed silver hair.

Even from a distance, it was evident that Cristo's smile didn't quite mask the tight features, nor the stiff, determined gait.

Solaris assumed something had gone amiss with the Cutting woman.

It was time for him to get to work.

"Your boss seems happy enough, eh?"

Captain Damien Stravos appeared beside Solaris. The man stroked his overgrown beard with his knuckles and squinted into the sun.

He was short for a Greek, his head not quite meeting Solaris's shoulder, with a rotund stomach that hung over bowed legs.

"And why not?" Solaris agreed without qualm. Deliberately, he studied the horizon where the blue sky merged with the deeper blue of the ocean. "It is a beautiful day today."

"Somehow, I do not think it is the weather that has put Cristo in a good mood," Stravos commented, wheezing, but from his excitement or his girth, Solaris wasn't sure. "We have made a good deal."

Solaris did not correct the captain. It was a good deal. The transportation of thirty tons of cocaine to the United States—a street value of millions—with the promise of more if all went well.

The risks were high, but that was the nature of their business. Solaris didn't agree with Delgado's plans for freighting the merchandise over the Caribbean Sea when smaller boats, while less profitable, were easier to keep under the DEA's radar.

But Solaris kept his opinion to himself. He had no stake in that side of Cristo's business, so the risk was not his.

Captain Stravos met Cristo at the top of the gangway. The latter ordered his men to stand guard by the rail several feet away.

"Good day, Damien."

"Yes, yes. A good day." The captain glanced at Solaris. "Were we not just talking about that?"

After Solaris shrugged, the men shook hands. "You are ready to finalize our plans?" Cristo asked.

"Yes, yes," Stravos responded once again, his voice more eager.

Something Solaris had thought impossible.

"How is your lovely wife, Cristo?"

"She is doing well. In fact, she insists on your dining with us the day after tomorrow."

"Fine, fine," he said, barely masking his joy.

Cristo Delgado bit back the irritation and widened his smile. It was no secret that Stravos lusted after his wife. But Cristo chose to ignore the fact. For now.

Stravos was annoying certainly, but he was an excellent captain. And he asked very few questions. Besides, it wasn't Stravos that sparked Cristo's impatience, it was the Cutting woman. And now, Calvin West.

"Allow me a moment with my man, here." Cristo nodded toward Solaris. "Then I will join you, Damien. For some brandy, maybe?"

"Of course." Stravos tipped his hat briefly, and then made his way to the bridge of the ship. "I will have someone return and escort you to my quarters."

Cristo waited a moment, his gaze settled on the sky just beyond Solaris's left shoulder. "You have the opportunity to take care of some unfinished business for me."

"What business?"

Cristo handed him the business card. "Calvin West has returned."

"West?" Solaris glanced at the card, surprised. His mind processed the implications. "Here?"

"He accompanied the Cutting woman."

"So your inside source was right." Solaris nodded, satisfied. "She came. Did she bring the MONGREL prototype?"

"We'll see soon enough."

"West was MI6 until last year. Now, I believe, he is some

sort of diplomatic liaison between London and Washington, D.C. Why is he involved?"

"It does not matter. He is an unexpected opportunity," Cristo answered. "You've been given another chance at West. Don't screw it up again. Understand?"

"I will take care of it," Solaris replied, pleased. "What about Jason Marsh?"

"Marsh is not your concern," Delgado retorted. "Find West. When you're done, bring the woman to me. If she's decided to visit her ex-husband, I will find out why, and how I can use her presence to my advantage. Then I'll dispose of her. You can do what you please to West. Just make sure of the impact. On both of them."

"I will." Solaris pocketed the card. "But if West let you know he was here, there's a good chance he has already set a plan in motion."

"You act as if I should care," Cristo said arrogantly, then walked away with a wave of his hand. "Just do your job this time, Solaris. I won't tolerate another failure."

Chapter Six

Shacks rose above the city of Caracas. Some burrowed into the hillsides while most balanced precariously on toothpick stilts. Painted in a rainbow of dingy pastels, they turned the slant of land into an eerie chessboard of light and shadows.

"Your sense of fashion and mine are quite different, Cal. But I'm learning to appreciate your style."

Julia stepped from the rented Jeep. She wore a black Lycra top and matching pants. Both fit like a second skin and were surprisingly comfortable.

Flecks of broken glass and torn papers flashed dimly in the spattering of yellow streetlights.

"Just stay focused. This isn't a place where you want to get distracted." Cal cast a sideways glance, his eyes resting a few moments on her freshly scrubbed features, the short ponytail, before skimming over the soft curve of her backside. "Or be distracting."

"Dutifully noted." Ignoring the flash of heat in her belly, she sidestepped the path of one particularly erratic rat that scampered across the narrow dirt road. A scurry of shadows burst from a nearby garbage pile. Revulsion slid up her back, worked the knot between her shoulders. "Who are we meeting?"

"A friend of Jason's." Cal took her elbow and steered her to the nearest shanty. A lime-green dwelling stood half buried in the hillside behind, its two small windows covered with newspaper.

"Charming," she murmured.

The front door swung open.

"Bloody hell, man. Did you have to leave my car in one of the worst areas in town?" Renalto demanded in a low, harsh voice. The man's black eyes darted up and down the road. "It was stripped almost to nothing by the time I got to it."

Julia stopped midstep, not sure what surprised her more, Renalto at the door or the British accent that tumbled from his mouth.

"It couldn't be helped. You'll get reimbursed." Cal grabbed her hand and pulled her into the shack.

"From who? Cain?" The operative snorted. "Not bloody likely. Especially after he hears that it was you, my friend, who messed up," Renalto complained and shut the door behind the couple. "You're not exactly on his top-agent list right now."

"Cain doesn't have a top-agent list," Cal commented dryly. "Only a 'those who owe me a favor' list."

Ignoring him, Renalto locked the door and punched in a code before placing a false wall over the keypad. "Besides, how would it look? I'm supposed to be a drug-addicted supplier. I never have enough money to repair my cab."

"Maybe as suspicious as a drug-addicted supplier with a state-of-the-art alarm system," Julia inserted mildly.

"You got me there." As Renalto smiled, his dark eyes swept over Julia in one lengthy, interested gaze. "Ms. Cutting, I apologize for the abrupt ending to our meeting earlier today."

"No more sorry than I am about your head. Is it better?"

"Much better."

Before Julia could stop him, Renalto took her fingers and brought them to his lips for a light kiss. "Now."

"Cut it out, Ren. The Don Juan act—"

"I'll bet Cal hasn't fed you anything," Renalto interrupted. His dark eyes flickered over her.

"No, he hasn't," she agreed slowly. "But we've been a little busy." As if on cue, her stomach rumbled.

"See what I mean?" After another quick kiss, he let go of her fingers. "You've come to the right place. I'll take care of you."

Julia glanced over the dimly lit room. Newspapers and clothes littered a broken-down sofa. Sweat and dirt stains tattooed the back cushions, darkening the dull beige upholstery. More magazines, papers and old food cartons lay strewn across liberally gouged black and white linoleum. The checkered floor slapped up against a set of shabby cabinets with only a microwave on top to serve as his kitchen.

When her eyes found Renalto's, he chuckled. "Don't let the looks of this sty deceive you."

He reached under the counter and flipped a toggle switch. Suddenly, the tiles of the floor lifted, then slid back revealing a four-foot-square opening.

"My true living quarters." Renalto indicated with a bow.

"Gracias." Charmed, she grinned. A broad grin that flashed an attractive dimple on one cheek.

Renalto's eyes widened. He placed his hand over his heart and staggered back. *"Dulce Jesús. Un ángel en la tierra."* Sweet Jesus. An angel on earth.

"Mía, Renalto," Cal snapped. Immediately he regretted his outburst. Julia's eyes shot to his.

Renalto whistled through his teeth, then he spoke again in English. "I did not understand, *amigo.* You have my apologies."

"Did not understand what?" Julia kept her expression curious while her heart picked up its beat.

Mine, Cal had said. She crossed her arms over her chest to stop her heart from knocking against her ribs.

She was fluent in several languages, including French, Mandarin and Spanish. A fact that had never come up in a conversation between her and Cal during their brief affair.

"I did not understand that this case was personal for him, too." Renalto laughed, a deep chuckle that did little to ease the tension. "Too bad. I make a rather good Valentino."

"Valentino?" Julia asked, her curiosity real now.

"The actor who was famous for his love for women," Renalto explained, then added without qualm. "I have an addiction to old movies."

Julia shook her head, amazed.

Renalto shot her a wolfish smile. "Maybe you'd be interested in seeing my collection sometime, eh?"

Julia laughed. "Maybe."

"Are you done?" Cal asked, his tone terse.

"Almost." With slow deliberation, Renalto winked at Julia before he turned back to Cal. "Now I'm done."

"Did you follow Jorgie?"

"Yes. Leopold's car was nearby," Renalto answered, his tone much lighter than his friend's. "I used it to follow them."

"Leopold?" Julia frowned, remembering. "The sky cap?"

"Leo's more of an associate. He just borrowed the uniform to help me when Cal notified me of your flight in."

"How did you know Delgado's men were going to jump us?" Julia asked Cal.

"A hunch," Cal answered, then turned to Renalto, dismissing her harshly enough to set her teeth on edge. "Where did they go?"

"Delgado keeps a *hacienda* on the other side of the city. They returned there," Renalto said, his eyebrow cocked just a bit at Cal's attitude. "But I saw nothing unusual. After a few hours, I left rather than chance being discovered. I don't know what you put on that card, but Jorgie hauled butt back to his master."

"I gave Delgado something to think about besides Julia and Jason."

"What?"

"Me," Cal said solemnly.

"No offense, West, but as much as Delgado has reason to hate you, it's nothing compared to how much he hates Jason," Renalto pointed out.

"What do you mean?" Julia asked. "Why does Delgado hate Jason? And you, Cal?"

"Jason has spent the last eight years of his life making Delgado miserable." Renalto considered his words. "I've only joined in the fun a year ago, but it didn't take more than an hour to understand this is a grudge match."

"What grudge?"

Renalto shrugged. "Whatever it was, Jason kept it from me."

"He kept it from everyone it seems," Cal commented; his eyes caught Julia's.

"Including me," she answered, surprised at how easy the lie slid off her tongue.

"Until recently, Jason had been in the States gathering intel," Renalto continued. "He must have gotten a hold of something big. He contacted me from Washington, said he needed my help. Then he told me he was on his way back here to bring Delgado down."

"He quit the agency."

"I know that now. My superiors told me after Jason disappeared." Renalto's smile turned cold. "But it doesn't make sense. Nothing on this earth was more important to Jason than that job."

"Something was," Cal answered with an arrogance that

slapped at Julia. "Greed. Or a lover. Or maybe even from fear for his life."

"I don't believe any of those reasons," Julia said out loud.

"Doesn't matter." Renalto grunted. "Delgado snatched Jason within days after he arrived. The poor bastard didn't have a chance."

"How did Delgado know he was coming?"

"Probably the same way he knew Julia was on the morning plane. He's got someone on the inside. I was told by my superiors to wait until Cal showed up. So here I am."

"You've had no word on Jason, then?" Cal prompted.

"I don't need it. I know Delgado." Renalto's brown eyes softened as they rested on Julia. "Jason disappeared ten days ago. It is better to pray that he is dead, because if he is alive—"

"We'll find out either way." Cal cut him off, but not before Julia noticed the grim tightening of his jaw. "Right now, I need intelligence on Esteban Alvarez. I want to meet with him."

"The ex-cartel partner?" Renalto thought for a moment. "He's hosting a huge party tomorrow at his villa. Rumor is, he's trying to go legit. There are quite a few important people on the invite list. People who don't want their friendship with a drug lord made public."

Cal's mouth flattened into a hard line. "That'll do."

"What are you planning—"

"Shh." Renalto cut off Julia. "Listen."

The crunch of dirt and stone penetrated the shanty.

Within moments both men flanked the window, their pistols in their hands.

"What is it?" Julia whispered.

"Tires on gravel," Renalto answered. "Lucy, we've got company."

"Stop quoting movies, Ren, or so help me—"

"It's a television show," Julia corrected absently, her eyes on the curtains. Waiting.

"I think I'm in love," Renalto whispered. "A woman who knows *I Love Lucy.*"

Headlights flashed through the windows. A moment later, car doors slammed closed.

Renalto moved the curtain aside slightly with the barrel of his gun. "Damn it, West. You were followed."

"The hell I was."

"Four headlights. Two cars full of black-suited dudes," Renalto observed. "They're not here for a tea party."

More doors slammed amidst a burst of masculine laughter.

"I knew it," Renalto bit out. "It's Jorgie and some more of Delgado's goons."

"What do we do?" Julia asked, her voice still a mere whisper. She kept her distance from the window. No use giving Jorgie an open target.

"The first car belongs to Leopold," Renalto realized aloud. "They're dumping something from the trunk."

Cal swore, then shifted closer to see for himself. "What is it?"

"A huge burlap sack."

Jorgie aimed his machine gun at the sack and fired several rounds into the burlap.

"Son of a bitch!" Renalto dove for the door. A moment later, Cal tackled him, pinning the other man to the floor.

"Let me up, damn it," Renalto raged.

"No." Grunting, Cal took an elbow in the gut, but kept his grip tight. If he didn't, they'd all be dead. "It's too late, Ren," he ordered, then said again softly. "If someone was in that bag, they're dead already."

Emotion played across Renalto's face: anger, disbelief, then finally acceptance and grief.

Renalto laid his head against the floor, then hit it with his forehead once, hard. "Bloody hell."

Julia crossed to the window. Cal heard her sharp intake of breath and was on his feet a moment later.

"Oh, my God," she breathed out the words. "Cal, hurry. Jorgie just threw a grenade into one of the cars."

"Get away from the window!" Cal reached for Julia. A split second later, the blast shook the air and filled it with dust and smoke. A huge fire ball burned where the car sat.

Flashes of orange and yellow lit up the inside of the trailer.

"Get down!" Cal pushed her to the floor, then covered her with his body.

"Renalto!" Jorgie yelled. "This is a warning. It's time you joined your friend."

Suddenly, gunfire ripped through paneling. Julia stifled a scream even as the wall and windows absorbed the impact.

"Bulletproof," Renalto yelled over another blast of ammunition. "They're going to figure it out soon enough."

"What the bloody hell were you thinking, going to the window?" Cal looked down, putting Julia's face only centimeters from his. "Of all the stupid things to do. If I ever see you standing in harm's way again—" Cal suppressed an oncoming shudder. He'd be damned if he'd let her see his torment.

"I got the message." She flinched, but didn't fight to get away from Cal.

He took the moment while his nerves quieted, his heartbeat settled back into a normal rhythm.

"They're grabbing more weapons," Renalto warned. "Hell, artillery is coming out of the trunk like it was Mary Poppins's bloody carpetbag."

"What do we do?"

He glanced at the opening in the floor. "Take cover."

Quickly, Cal stood with Julia in his arms.

"Get ready," he warned, a split second before he dropped her through the trapdoor to the room below.

"Here it comes!" Renalto punched the switch.

Both men dove into the hole. The door slid closed over their heads.

"Cover your ears!"

Julia dropped to the cement floor. Pain jarred her backside. She bit back a small cry and slapped her palms over her ears.

The shack exploded above them. Dirt and smoke clogged the air, choked off her oxygen. She coughed, felt the burn of gunpowder in her lungs.

"Breathe through your nose. Short but slow. Use your shirt to cover your lower face," Cal ordered, but this time he didn't hold her.

Julia did as Cal instructed. Small amounts of oxygen opened her airway. She coughed again but this time only grit scratched at the back of her throat. "What was that?"

"Grenade launcher," Cal stated, then grabbed Julia's arm and pulled her from the floor. "We won't be able to get out of here easily. Which will make us sitting ducks."

"Since their usual tactics include broken limbs and decapitations, I'll consider myself lucky," Renalto sneered.

Renalto stepped to the back wall and opened a panel behind one of the bricks. "Let them come in after us then. I'll more than match their firepower."

He punched in a code. Suddenly, a small door slid open.

Renalto flipped the light switch, revealing a fifteen-by-ten room just beyond the doorway. "It's built into the hill behind the shack."

An artillery of weapons covered a floor-to-ceiling shelving unit on the far wall of the room. On the opposite side stood a small kitchen complete with a four-foot counter and a set of rusted bar stools. A small army cot was set up a short distance away in the far right corner.

Julia noted the bed was made—its blanket and sheets tucked and tight and army issued. Above the cot were several boxed shelves filled with DVDs, but it was the set of six security monitors mounted on the wall beside the bed that caught Julia's attention.

"It's not much but it's home," Renalto explained as he grabbed for an automatic machine gun. *"Say hello to my little friend."*

"That's a bad imitation of Pacino. And *Scarface* wasn't that great of a movie. He died at the end." Cal crossed to his friend in three quick strides. "All of this artillery Kate's doing?"

"Yes." Renalto placed the gun back on the rack and grabbed a lighter Uzi. "What can I say, *amigo?* She has a soft spot for me."

Cain's sister was in charge of the Labyrinth technical division. And from the arsenal of weapons and intelligence equipment, she excelled at her job.

"So you work for Labyrinth, also. Not the DEA," Julia commented. Even with her limited knowledge, she identified at least three AK-47s, a few sharp-shooting rifles, some grenades and flash bombs.

"Wouldn't be caught dead working for Cain MacAlister's group," Renalto admitted, his words hard—not quite jesting—but not harsh. More from the situation than anything, Julia realized. "Labyrinth agents are wimps. They're in and out. Quick operations."

"Quick results," Cal corrected, not offended. Cal helped himself to a couple of extra clips of ammo.

"In the DEA we go undercover for years," Renalto continued, his lips twisted in scathing humor. "Churn out the bad guys from the trenches. What do you do?"

"I was told recently that our job is to save the world,"

Cal answered derisively. "For king and country. No middle ground. No matter what it takes. Or who it destroys."

"Cal, look." Renalto pointed to a nearby surveillance screen. Jorgie and his men stepped into their cars. Both engines gunned. The wheels spit out gravel as the cars raced down the hillside.

"Didn't even stay for dessert." Renalto lifted the Uzi and settled its barrel in the hollow of his shoulder. "Cowards."

Julia watched the cars for a moment, then focused on the other screens. "Where are your neighbors? Don't they care that their street has been invaded?"

"I have several neighbors, but they aren't stupid," Renalto explained, surprised. "Most douse their lights and pretend they aren't home. Otherwise, they might draw the attention of the wrong people."

"We still need to get out of here," Cal observed. He gestured toward the outer room. "Only way."

"Yep. The downside of living in a hole."

"Stay here," Cal told Julia. "We need to clear a path to the outside. Once we open the ceiling, all hell's going to break loose."

Before she could answer, he grabbed an extinguisher from a nearby shelf and headed through the door to the outer area.

At Cal's nod, Renalto hit the switch. The trap door opened and fiery debris fell through. Almost instantly, smoke filled the room. Cal hit fiery wreckage with white foam.

It took them almost an hour to clear the mess of tangled steel and charred remains.

When Julia worked her way out of the cellar room, she saw Cal's friend kneeling on the ground, Leopold's car ablaze behind him.

Renalto took a knife from his boot and sliced the bag open. A shock of gray hair shone in the light of the flames.

Sickened, Julia walked slowly toward the men, trying to keep her knees from buckling.

Leopold. Delgado's men had killed Leopold and dumped him at Renalto's doorstep.

What had Jason gotten her into?

"You're going to get the hell out of here," Cal ordered Renalto. "You have no idea what information Leopold gave them. If they find out you're alive, they'll come after you."

"Leopold knew very little about me. He'd have given them nothing of importance."

Renalto stood and studied the burning car, not really seeing it. "They beat him with a bat or something. Probably didn't even ask him a question. Just took him off the street and beat him to death."

"You couldn't have stopped them, Ren," Cal warned quietly. "Delgado prefers his employees had family, more specifically, family who lives in South America. Collateral damage for those who strayed or screwed up. It's easier for a person to risk their own life, but almost impossible when it's their family."

Something vile and dark slid through Julia.

Cal glanced down at Leopold. "Delgado knows I'm on the offensive. We need a shift in power to throw him off a bit. The best way to do that is to stick to our operation."

"What operation?" Renalto questioned.

"We're going to find Jason," Cal answered, his voice dead of emotion.

Renalto let out a short, bitter laugh. "Don't get me wrong, Cal. I've definitely got a personal stake in this now. But we can't just walk into Cristo Delgado's territory and take back one of our own. It would be suicide."

"Not suicide, but definitely tricky," Cal admitted grimly. "Cain had enough pull to get me the floor plans to Delgado's main villa. If Jason isn't there, it's possible we'll find evidence to his whereabouts. It's the best we got right now."

"All right. I'm in," Renalto conceded. "Delgado's main residence is in the jungle. A villa in Sierra de Perijá, on the Colombian border. Hell, it's more of a compound or a prison, really. Twenty-foot walls of imported granite surround the damn thing. Four stories of house with terra-cotta tiles and columns."

Cal nodded. "He also has a state-of-the-art security system. Lasers, motion detectors, cameras and armed guards with attack dogs."

"Delgado runs his empire from there. His wife and son are prisoners most of the time, kept under intense security. They leave only on Sundays. And only then for church service at a Jesuit mission called *Santuario de la flor.* Shrine of the Little Flower. It's located only a few miles from the villa."

"How long would it take you to get me the list of personnel at the compound, their schedules and any delivery service schedules?"

Renalto took a moment, then sighed. "Without risk of discovery? A few days. Not giving a damn? Less than twelve hours."

"Make it a day," Cal said. "I don't care if Delgado finds out, but not before we find what we need."

"I'll arrange it, *amigo.*" Renalto spit on the ground. "But I want to return Leopold to his family first."

"All right," Cal agreed, then thought for a moment. "Do you have access to a plane, Ren?"

"Might be able to get my hands on one."

"Do it then."

"You're thinking of flying right up to his door?"

"No, only to the front porch," Cal replied, then nodded at Renalto's underground bunker. "How are you fixed for supplies?"

"I have most of what we need on the shelves and I can pick up the rest," he remarked. "And if you want to get that close, I'm bringing the whole bloody arsenal. We're going to need it."

"Good. We'll meet up late tomorrow afternoon."

"You'll find me at the old hangar on the farthest side of the airport," Renalto offered, his voice edged with equal resolve. "I'll be waiting."

"Don't do anything stupid, Renalto."

"I won't," the other man promised. His gold tooth flashed beneath the hard line of his mouth. "While I'm ferreting out the information, what are you going to do?"

"Get some sleep. I haven't had more than two hours in the last forty-eight," Cal answered. He looked once again at Leopold. "Tomorrow, I'm going to visit an old friend."

"*We're* going to visit an old friend," Julia stated firmly.

"Yes, *we* are." Cal studied her for a moment. "Don't worry, Julia, your presence at this meeting is required."

TWO HOURS LATER, JULIA HAD gained very little information on the meeting Cal had planned the next day.

Before he took a shower, Cal had ordered Julia not to answer the door. To stay close to the bedroom. To stay away from the balcony and windows.

If he'd told her where his gun was, she thought, she'd probably shoot him.

Unsettled, she wandered into the bedroom where earlier in the day, she'd put her things away.

While the living room held a comfortable mixture of feminine and masculine decor, the bedroom—though subtle and sophisticated—definitely leaned more toward the latter.

Rich tones of plum and chocolate draped broad windows in a blend of silk and cotton. The colors softened the rustic, pine furniture, making the room inviting. She ran her hand over a nearby dresser, enjoying the texture of the rough old wood, the grooves and scratches brought on by time.

A corner fireplace of mosaic tile added to the appeal. On a cold evening, a warm fire would turn the atmosphere from cozy to romantic, she imagined.

"Nice place, wrong man," Julia murmured.

She opened the top drawer, expecting to find it empty like the armoire where she'd hung her new clothes. Instead, sweaters of different colors and styles filled the space.

The subtle scent of clean citrus and warm, oriental spices filled the air, catching Julia off guard.

Julia dug through the sweaters until she discovered a small green bottle at the bottom of the drawer.

A quick sniff confirmed her suspicions. Jason's cologne.

Anger hit with the force of a sharp smack across her cheek, but it was the feeling of betrayal that nearly dropped her to her knees.

Calvin brought her to Jason's apartment. Struggling for a clear head, Julia glanced back at the connecting bathroom. The sound of the shower running was muffled, but there.

Julia swung the door in and shoved the shower curtain aside. "This is Jason's apartment, isn't it?" Betrayal fed the hurt beneath her heart, but determination kept it from her voice. "I found this."

Slowly, Cal turned the faucet off and grabbed a towel from the nearby rack. He glanced at the bottle.

"It shouldn't matter." Not bothering to dry himself, he draped the towel over his hips.

"I'll decide for myself what matters, West."

"What difference does it make?" He stepped past her and through the bathroom doorway.

She followed him into the bedroom. "Damn it, Cal. Why didn't you tell me?"

"This wasn't his home, Julia. It was a safe house set up off the radar when he was in the country."

Turning his back to her, he rummaged through the dresser's middle drawer and pulled out a white pair of boxer briefs.

"Which was a damn sight more than he was in the States," she added.

"It was the best place to bring you on such short notice. It's untraceable." He started to untie his towel, then stopped when she didn't turn around.

She crossed her arms and waited.

With a shrug, he dropped the towel that hung low on his waist and stepped into the briefs.

"That doesn't answer my question," she insisted, willing her eyes to stay open, the groan to stay deep in her chest. Julia couldn't stop herself from watching. It always struck her as one of the more intimate, almost sexual parts of their relationship. Dressing in front of one another.

"Why didn't you tell me Jason lived here?" She tucked her hair behind her ear and widened her stance.

"Maybe I wanted to avoid this type of conversation," Cal answered, damning himself for not clearing out Jason's belongings.

"What the hell is that supposed to mean?" The moist heat clung to her curves, caused the cotton pajamas to stick to her skin.

Cal took in the simple yellow cotton camisole tee, the scrubbed features with just enough pink in her cheeks to validate the rage that flashed sharp in her eyes. But it was the dozens of little pink and yellow flowers stretched across cotton pajama pants, the drawstring waistband sitting low on her hips that sparked a familiar heat in his blood.

"It means…" Annoyed, Cal wiped some of the water from his face with the towel. "Knowing you were staying in this apartment, an apartment that he *used* would only kick your feelings into overdrive."

"The only thing I'm emotional about right now, is the fact that you're withholding information."

The slight hitch in her voice rippled through Calvin. He froze, hearing the vulnerable edge he'd only heard once before. *Bloody hell.* "Let it go, Julia."

The ripple morphed into a fast-paced hum that set his back teeth on edge. The anger, the desire, the exhaustion moved against him in rolling waves, breaking down the barriers he needed to keep her at bay.

"I did once." Suddenly, they weren't talking about the apartment anymore; they were talking about the betrayal a year ago. "I can't now. Too much is at stake."

"Too much is at stake," he repeated, a sad twist set across his lips. He stepped in to her. Without thought, his hand reached up and cupped her cheek, his eyes locked on to hers. "More than you know." He whispered the words, the hum now volts of desire shooting through his nerves, his blood. "You brought me into this to help you. Now, the question is, can you trust me to do my job?"

"Trust is not part of this deal. Your job was to protect me, nothing more." She'd thought the humiliation of it was part of her past. She'd been wrong. Tears pricked at her eyes, but she refused to give in to the pain that brought them there. Wrong about many things.

"The hell it is—"

Suddenly, she found herself set away from Calvin.

Cal grabbed his buzzing cell phone from his pants' pocket and hit the button. "West."

"It's Cain." The tone was abrupt, irritated.

"I've got the information on that recording you left me," Cain said without preamble. "There was nothing else on the memory. The words stopped before she shut off the recorder."

"Are you sure?"

"Yes," Cain snapped. "And the voice on the recorder isn't Delgado's."

Cal took a moment to process that. He glanced at Julia, saw the hint of a smirk. Clever girl. "One of his men?"

"No. When we found out it wasn't Delgado, I had some of my men do a little leg work."

Curiosity tempered the desire. "And?"

"It's her apartment's security guard. A man by the name of Curtis Matthews. Julia paid him a hundred dollars to make the recording for her."

"Curtis Matthews," Cal said, remembering. "A grandpa-type who's counting the days until his retirement, so he can live off his pension."

Without a word, Julia turned on her heel and walked over to the bed.

"That's him," Cain confirmed. "You know what this means, right?"

"Yes," Cal replied, his eyes pinned to Julia on the bed, his tone razor sharp. "Time for some answers."

CAIN MACALISTER HEARD THE CLICK on the phone line. "Damn fool hung up on me."

"Did you expect anything else?"

"No." Cain hit the off button on the speakerphone, then leaned back into the high-backed leather chair. "All right, Jon. I did what you asked me to do, now tell me why the hell I did it?"

A small smile tugged at the corner of the older man's mouth. While Cain and Calvin were friends, old man Mercer understood his own relationship with Cain went far beyond. Jon Mercer had once been Cain's boss, and now he was his advisor, confidant and sometimes even surrogate parent.

"Calvin will take care of Julia, Cain. Trust me. He's the

best one for the job." President Mercer leaned back into his chair, white eyebrows drawn together with concern. "He'll keep her alive, even if she's determined to get herself killed."

"And the MONGREL?"

"If she knows where it is, we won't find it until she's ready for us, too," Jon reasoned. "Damn, the girl is smart."

Cain heard the underlining thread of pride running through the older man's comment.

"Too smart for her own good," Cain retorted.

"Maybe. But the ten million dollar hoax did the trick, didn't it?"

"How did you know there wasn't any ransom money?"

"Educated guess. Once we knew the ransom demand was a decoy, there'd be no reason for her to take any money."

Cain grunted. He trusted the old man's instincts more than anyone else's. Jon Mercer spent a decade of his life hip deep in jungle scum, driving out the Viet Cong. "I have to admit, if she didn't work for you—"

"You can't have her for Labyrinth," Jon interrupted, chuckling. "So get the thought out of your head."

"Well, you might have to share her with a federal penitentiary if she's tried for treason." But there was very little force behind the threat. Whether he liked it or not, Julia Cutting was family. Jon Mercer's family.

"It won't come to that." Jon dismissed the notion with a wave of his hand. "I have enough favors to call in, but it will mess up her life a bit."

"Well, from what I've seen of Julia Cutting, she doesn't shy away from big messes."

"LET'S HAVE IT, JULIA."

"What?"

"The truth, damn it!" Cal snapped the phone closed, then tossed it onto the bed in front of her.

"You first," she retorted.

"Look, you've got ten seconds to start explaining why your security guard pretended to be Cristo Delgado."

"You had the recording analyzed?" She stood, giving herself a little more advantage. "Don't tell me you didn't *trust* me, Cal."

"Your time is running out." Without warning, he reached out and snagged her arm and yanked her toward him. When she gasped, his fingers tightened. Anger whipped through her, setting her jaw and shoulders rigid. "Didn't you just lecture me about full disclosure?"

"I had to be sure you would bring me with you. If you thought I was in danger—"

"You knew I was going to Caracas," he interrupted. "How?"

"Jon Mercer pulled your and Jason's files. He went around me and through Cain's secretary so I wouldn't be alerted. When I found out, I did a little investigating."

"Investigating?"

Julia blew out a breath. "I went through Jon Mercer's desk and briefcase."

"And the story about you finding the files in your apartment?"

"Not true."

"Which answers why you weren't abducted by Delgado's men."

"Yes."

"So once you found the files, you assumed I would be put on Jason's case?"

"No. I just knew that you owed Jason. President Mercer hadn't made any notations regarding you, so there was no way for me to know you'd been assigned, other than your file had been pulled," Julia admitted. "Did they know about the favor you owed Jason?"

"No," Cal lied, but a small pinch of guilt forced him to drop his hold on her. In truth, Cain decided the favor gave Cal the perfect cover to get close to Jason in order to terminate him if necessary. Jason would believe Cal's intentions were honorable and give him a chance to get close to him, find out where the MONGREL is located.

"A coincidence?" she asked, her eyes searching his.

"Not really. While I was MI6, I spent quite an amount of time in the jungles of South America. Mercer and Cain had knowledge of this. It made me the perfect solution to their problem. But do you know the collateral damage you could have caused with these lies?" Cal demanded. "Jason's life if he is, in fact, still alive. Your life. A half dozen other people?"

"I have a good idea. But it was a risk I had to take."

"I bet." Cal leaned against the dresser and crossed his arms. "And the money that was left on your coffee table?"

"There is no account with ten million in it."

His face stayed impassive. "Tell me something I don't know, sweetheart."

"You knew?"

"I suspected when Cain told me he couldn't trace the funds. It's much easier to find something when you know it exists. When he couldn't locate the missing money or a new account, I drew the logical conclusion."

"Good for you," she said wryly.

"So how did Delgado know you were on your way?"

"I don't know," Julia said honestly. "I've only told you."

"But Jason was the one who brought you into this, wasn't he?" Cal's back teeth slammed together, his neck muscles contracted until they were rigid. "Bloody hell. I should've known. The bastard."

"Are you trying to tell me that Jason set me up? That he told Delgado I was on my way?" She shook her head. "That isn't possible. I was only supposed to contact Delgado if I couldn't get Jason out any other way."

"Run that past me again? Did you say you were planning on contacting Delgado?"

Rage whipped around Cal. For the first time, Julia identified the man who hunted others in the jungle. "If all else failed, Cal," she defended.

"And since you don't have the ten million," Cal said slowly. "What were you going to use as a trade?"

But he already knew. Deep down he just knew.

"The MONGREL," Julia admitted quietly.

"How in the hell did you get a hold of the MONGREL?"

"I don't actually have it," Julia admitted.

"But you know where it is?"

"No," she evaded, settling for the half-truth. She had a good idea but wasn't ready to share that information. "Or at least I'm not sure."

Cal stepped in, forcing her to look up at him. "Did Jason also tell you *why* he stole the technology?"

"Insurance. A bargaining chip, maybe. The conversation was frantic. He was late for his flight to Caracas." She rubbed her forehead, trying to feign the beginnings of a headache. "It had taken me the first few minutes to register the fact that it was him. I hadn't talked to him in so long."

Cal grabbed her hand and yanked it away from her temple. "You don't really think I'm going to fall for that load of garbage, sweetheart. I know bloody well you remembered every single syllable Jason uttered. Your mind is trained to, otherwise you wouldn't be working for Jon."

"You're going to have to, Cal, because that's all I got." She flopped back onto the bed. More for distance than defiance.

"Have you ever been here before?"

"No."

"Did you ever talk about coming here with Jason?"

"Never." Julia propped back on her elbows.

"No aunt or uncle who could be living close by that he wanted you to meet?"

"We didn't have that kind of relationship, Cal," Julia replied. "I even thought about calling his parents, but they know less about their son than I do. And I was only married to him for a few years."

"Most of which he spent out in the field," Cal commented. "Isn't that why you divorced him?"

"No," Julia answered, suddenly tired of hiding from the truth. "He divorced me."

Cal's head snapped around.

"He divorced me." Humiliation filled her, making the words taste bitter. "Then he ran off to join the DEA."

"You're being a little dramatic, don't you think? You make it sound like DEA was some kind of French Foreign Legion."

"To him I think it was. DEA, Labyrinth, MI6. Aren't they all the same?"

Cal caught the double-edged accusation in her words. "I was your lover, not your husband. Big difference."

"The only difference was that I gave Jason nothing the short time we were married. It took me a long time to realize that, but I did, eventually. When you came into my life, I thought I had it figured out. Thought I knew what love was about," she explained, her throat tight from embarrassment. But it was better to get it out in the open. "I was wrong."

"We were wrong, Julia. It would have never worked."

"I guess we finally agree on something."

"I guess we do." With nothing more to say, he turned away. "You take the bed, I'll grab the couch."

"And in the morning?"

"We save Jason."

Chapter Seven

Esteban Alvarez stood at the top of the terrace stairs and observed the scene before him. In the center of the back courtyard lay a long rectangular pool. Its underwater lights set the water glowing in a clear sheet of glass that seemingly hung suspended just on the horizon, where pool blurred into ocean. When one took a closer look, the water fell into a silent waterfall that flowed to a smaller pool just below.

Tikis on the lawn perimeter and small white lights looped through the trees cast the party in an intimate glow. An orchestra played background music. A little Chopin, Esteban noted. The conductor wouldn't pick up the pace until after Esteban greeted his guests and set the party in motion.

"Hello, Esteban."

"Ah, Tessa. I'm glad you decided to join me tonight."

"It's my job, darling," Tessa acknowledged with a slight smile.

Just this side of thirty, Tessa Reynar's features were flawless, classical. Her eyes blue, her hair the lightest shade of blond. With curves that Aphrodite would envy, she enticed men by simply walking past.

Satin, the color of sapphires, shimmered over her body, leaving one shoulder and arm covered, the other completely bare.

"I brought you some champagne." She handed him one of the two flutes she was holding.

Tessa had worked for him since the attempted assassination on his life four years ago. Originally a hospital administrator where he'd been admitted, she worked her way through channels and managed a small meeting with him just before he'd been discharged.

At first, he'd thought only to bed her until he listened to her proposed deal. Instead, she impressed him and soon became his business manager. She insisted on a professional relationship only. In return, she promised to double his income in a year and turn him into a legitimate businessman in five, if he wished.

His income was more than doubled. And while Tessa was beautiful, Esteban was intelligent himself and chose not to mix business with pleasure. Physical pleasure came and went, but a brilliant strategist and business manager was worth their weight in gold.

"Cal West is back in Caracas," he said casually, but his eyes sharpened, looking for a reaction. "With Jason Marsh's ex-wife."

"Really?" Tessa took a sip of her champagne. "When did they arrive?" She knew better than to ask how he'd come by the information.

"Yesterday," Esteban admitted.

"That was stupid of Mr. West," Tessa commented. "Does Cristo know?"

"Yes. But they found out the hard way." Esteban waved to a nearby couple. "Cristo's men tried to pick her up today, but West interfered with their plans."

"Is the woman alive?"

Esteban laughed. "Do I care?"

"Yes." She paused. "Because anything that involves Cristo interests you. Especially since he is holding a high-level DEA agent as prisoner and the repercussions of that could affect our plans if President Mercer decides to get testy over one of his own."

"Darling," Esteban responded. "I don't think I like the fact you know me so well."

"There's something else I know," she continued. "The one thing that sets you apart from your *friend,* Cristo, is the fact you remain civilized."

"And look where it got me," Esteban commented and touched the scar on his throat.

"An empire?" Tessa quipped. "Face it, Esteban. Ever since you took that bullet in the throat, everything you touch turns to gold."

"Maybe. But there is more to life than money."

"Spoken by a man who has lots of money."

He laughed and offered her his arm. "Enough talk about business tonight. I have guests that need attending."

She slipped her hand up and around the crook of his elbow, then followed him down the stairs.

After a brief glance from Esteban, the conductor turned the waltz into an introduction.

Immediately, the men and women turned their eyes to the couple on the bottom step of the terrace stairs. Esteban waited until a hush settled over the crowd, the applause to cease. "Ladies and gentlemen. I would like to thank you for coming to my little get-together."

Several Americans—politicians and other less public, yet influential, people—mingled with the South Americans. All at ease by the absence of paparazzi or those who would betray their secrecy.

Esteban raised his fluted glass to the crowd. "To new beginnings," he boomed.

Across the way, just on the edge of the thick of palm trees, Tessa caught the glint of glass, the smirk on a very attractive mouth before a couple stepped from the line of trees.

"You have two unexpected guests," she observed and tilted her champagne flute toward those same trees. "Once again, you don't have to put much effort into getting what you want, darling."

"What do you mean?"

"Calvin West just made an appearance at your party. And if I'm not mistaken, the lady with him is Julia Cutting."

Esteban followed Tessa's gaze, then stiffened in surprise. "He is an arrogant son of a bitch, isn't he? Doesn't he know half these people will recognize him here?"

"The recognition is mutual, I believe," Tessa stated. "Maybe he's willing to cross over to the dark side."

Esteban studied the woman. He'd seen her before, mostly in the background of Jon Mercer's press junkets. But never with her hair down in soft, short waves and her body encased in slim-fitting, thigh-high silk, the color of ripe blueberries and supported only by two delicate shoulder ties.

"Calvin West walking on the dark side?" Esteban mused. "Maybe. We'll find out soon enough. Along with a few other things."

"What other things?"

"For starters, I want to know how in the hell he got past my security."

"This is an unexpected pleasure." Esteban sat back in the couch and crossed his legs. His words, raspy, ground like steel shavings against his vocal cords.

One of Esteban's guards patted Cal down. But when he stepped toward Julia, Cal blocked his path.

"You can forego that formality, Stefan. I don't think you have to worry about Miss Cutting," Esteban ordered quietly.

Relieved when the guard stepped away, Julia let Cal take her elbow and lead her farther into the living room.

"Please, sit down. Make yourselves at home." He inclined

his head to the love seat across from him and waited for the couple to settle in. "I assume it won't be necessary to take precautions by handcuffing you both or something."

"If it is, then I might as well not offer them anything to drink, Esteban," Tessa commented, walking into the room.

"Hello," she said with a smile to the room in general, then slid onto the arm of a nearby leather chair. "Anyone thirsty?"

"Of course. I'll take my usual, darling," Esteban acknowledged. "Mr. West, Ms. Cutting, may I introduce my…business manager, Tessa Reynar."

"Hello." Julia held out her hand.

Smiling, Tessa shook it. "Hello again."

Intuitively, Julia understood the greeting was sincere and responded with her own smile.

Cal only flickered a brief look in her direction. No hands were offered, and no offense was taken.

"How about those drinks?" Tessa asked, then walked to the fully stocked bar in the corner of the library.

"We aren't staying that long," Cal replied. "You have something I need, Alvarez. Something I need bad enough to negotiate with the devil for."

"I being the devil, I take it," Esteban commented wryly.

Tessa laughed as she sauntered back, then handed a dark beer to Esteban. "Did you think otherwise, Esteban?"

He took a cigar from the mahogany box that Tessa offered. "Thank you, my dear."

"Would you like one, Mr. West?" Tessa asked, showing him the box.

"No, thank you."

"Having served as a diplomat a few years back for your British government, West, I would assume you would be a little better at negotiating. Using the words 'need bad enough,' could put you at a disadvantage." Esteban snipped off the end of his cigar. "Wouldn't you agree, Tessa?"

"Oh, I think Mr. West is a man who does very well for himself. Exactly how many men do you know could crash your dinner party, Esteban, and then find himself having drinks with you less than a half an hour later?"

"Touché, my dear." Esteban lit the cigar and took a few short puffs before he relaxed once again. "My curiosity has gotten the better of me on occasion, hasn't it? Cristo would have had you tortured the moment you stepped foot on the lawn, West. But then again, he's a barbarian."

"What if I told you I can give you the opportunity of a lifetime?"

Esteban stared at the end of his cigar. "I'm listening."

"President Mercer could become your ally," Cal replied. "I have the means to make it happen."

"You're serious?" Tessa asked.

"Very," Cal replied.

Esteban laughed. "I'm guessing you are not a man with a humanitarian nature, Mr. West, so what do you want in exchange for your matchmaking abilities. Money?"

"I want you to keep Julia under your protection for the next week or so."

"What?" Julia jumped from her couch. "Are you insane?"

Esteban laughed again, at her reaction or the suggestion, Julia couldn't be sure. "I'd have to agree with Ms. Cutting, here. You realize that you are placing the personal secretary of the United States President under the protection of—and as much as I hate the term—a drug lord."

"That's exactly what I am proposing," Cal said.

"No." Julia managed to keep the word low, but the edge was razor sharp. "I told you that I needed to go with you—"

"And I told you that wasn't happening," Cal bit back. "Delgado has shown his hand. He isn't going to kill Jason until he gets what he wants from him." Cal's eyes locked with the drug lord's. "Well?"

"You've heard that Esteban is trying to go legitimate, haven't you?" Tessa summarized, then turned to Esteban. "What better way to add to your credibility, than to keep Ms. Cutting safe from Cristo? President Mercer would be in your debt."

"It is an interesting prospect." Esteban sat back into his chair and rubbed a finger at the side of his nose. "But before I consider it, I have a few questions."

"I expected you would."

"Why do you want Jason Marsh? He's been compromised already."

"A personal matter."

"One I'll have to insist you share, Mr. West."

Cal's jaw worked its muscles for a good ten seconds, then he nodded his acceptance. "Ten years ago, Jason was to Delgado what Jorgie is now—head of Delgado's security—when an attempt was made on Delgado's life."

"I remember. He was shot two days after I received this." Esteban pointed to his throat.

"I'm sure you do. Some even said you were behind it. A sort of payback because of your near-death experience."

"They are mistaken. It was a vendetta hit, by a smaller cartel. Their leader thought to strike while the Trifecta was diluted. If I had gone after Cristo, he'd be dead," Esteban answered matter-of-factly. "But I had no reason to. There was no hard evidence that Cristo was behind the attempt on my life."

"Delgado spent three days in the hospital recovering from his gunshot wounds. I was sent in to finish off Delgado while he was weakened."

"Just Delgado?" Esteban asked, his eyes narrowing.

"No. I was sent in to kill you, too," Cal admitted wryly. "But my cover was blown before I even stepped foot off the plane. We had a mole in our house."

"And how does Jason fit in this scenario?"

"He saved my life."

"So you owe him. Simple enough," Tessa stated, then glanced at Julia. "Or maybe not."

"Does not matter, my dear. Somehow I believe Mr. West is sincere." Esteban put out his cigar. "The day before Jason Marsh disappeared, he called me. And, just like you, he offered me an opportunity." The drug lord's tone remained casual but his gaze sharpened. "He offered me technology."

"Go on," Cal replied evenly.

"I believe your government calls it the MONGREL," Esteban said. "Marsh agreed to give me the device in exchange for Delgado's dead body. I had to turn him down, of course."

"Because Delgado is a friend."

Esteban's laugh was harsh, sandpaper against his larynx. "No. We are not friends, but we do neighbor each other's territory and that makes the situation…difficult."

Tessa placed her hand on his shoulder. Without thinking, Esteban patted it.

"I didn't take Marsh up on his offer simply because I wouldn't have been able to keep the damn device," Esteban continued. "Not if I wanted Jonathon Mercer to believe I am turning legitimate."

"You could have taken it, then returned it to Mercer."

"Mercer would never have believed I hadn't stolen it and examined it first. He would've intensified his efforts to bring me down."

"Still, we might have all been better off if you had taken Jason Marsh's deal, darling," Tessa murmured.

"The question is, why would Marsh steal from his own government in order to secure Cristo's death?"

"I have no idea," Cal answered honestly. "And since I don't have the MONGREL, you'll have to settle for the good word

I will put in with President Mercer about your cooperation with this situation."

"I have to think about this, West. The ramifications, the rewards." Esteban leaned back. "Admittedly, you are making this difficult for me to refuse."

"Revenge and a shortcut to legitimacy. All for a little protection," Cal pointed out. "Too many people in the government are on Cristo's payroll. Only you have the trusted manpower to keep Julia safe."

Esteban glanced at Tessa. "What do you think, my dear?"

"I think he's either a hell of a negotiator or that he's in love with her." Tessa studied Cal for a moment, thoughtful. "Or both."

Chapter Eight

"I'm not going with Alvarez. I don't care if he did agree." Julia's fatigue morphed into nervous energy. One that pricked her temper. "Why didn't you tell me about this plan before?"

"I didn't have time."

Julia made a pithy remark.

Cal's head snapped around, with eyes narrowed.

"Care to run that past me again?"

"Not really," she replied blithely. "But it seems to me this idea stemmed from our argument last night."

"And if it did?"

Silently she cursed the humiliation that bristled the back of her neck. "There's no justification in leaving me behind. I have an invested interest here, Cal. Whether you like it or not."

"I don't have to justify anything, Julia. What I'm trying to do is complete this operation. Renalto and I need to move quickly. You'd slow us down."

"You seem to keep forgetting Delgado thinks I have the MONGREL."

"Don't fool yourself, Esteban does, too," Cal warned. "And no matter what he said, I'm sure he was more than willing to make that deal with Jason. Legitimacy or not, Esteban isn't a stupid man. Jason just disappeared before Esteban could finalize the agreement."

"You knew this before you decided to knock out half of Esteban's security team with Renalto's stun darts?"

"That's about it," Cal responded. "It's imperative to free Jason before Cristo Delgado realizes you have nothing. You stay with Alvarez and keep out of my way."

"You were telling Esteban the truth, weren't you? You owed Jason because he saved your life."

"I owe a lot of people, Julia," he admitted without qualm. "Not just Jason."

"Somehow this was different. This went far beyond a political or even an occupational favor. He told me to go to you. He wanted you to protect me."

"Which brings us back to your relationship with your ex-husband."

She ignored him. "He trusts you, Cal. Why?"

"Not enough to tell me about the mess he's gotten himself into." Cal rubbed his hands over his face and for the first time, Julia noted the tired lines.

"We weren't friends," Cal continued. "You can't be when you're…involved with the same woman."

"Jason and I weren't involved. It never went that deep."

"That, he did tell me."

Her head snapped up, her gaze pinned his. "When?"

"A few weeks after we parted ways, I ran into him at one of the D.C. bars. An English bar, owned by one of my father's friends," Cal explained. "I'd been drinking. He accused me of playing emotional games with you. Then proceeded to beat the hell out of me."

She remembered seeing Cal shortly after. The bruised cheek, the split lip. A mission gone bad, he'd told her. "Did you fight back?"

"No," Cal admitted. "Believe it or not, there's a certain code men follow."

"One that forces you to get beaten by an ex-husband?"

"At the time I agreed with him." Cal stepped toward her until only a few inches separated them. "You were a target. Nothing more, nothing less. But even I recognized that using you to gain access to your computer...was crossing a line."

Surprised, Julia simply stared at him. Cal had never admitted to anything so human.

"Why you?" she asked. If she didn't go with him, she'd have to tell him about Jason's son, Argus. Despite her promise to Jason.

"Cain could have sent anyone in. How did you end up on this operation, Cal?"

"Jason went rogue a few months after our run-in at the bar. Cain realized only after the MONGREL prototype had disappeared. Because Jason helped develop the device, he became the primary suspect."

"Jason isn't a traitor." She dismissed the thought as absurd. He would have never turned over that kind of device to a drug lord. "That still doesn't explain why Cain sent you. Unless he knew that Jason had saved your life."

"Cain didn't base his decision on that. We both understood Jason wouldn't hesitate to kill me if he thought I was there to blow his deal," Cal replied. "Cain was aware that I had a... more personal connection...with Jason."

"Personal connection?" Her head snapped up, saw the answer in Cal's face. "Me."

"You said you loved me," Cal explained. "Cain was aware Jason knew."

"But only you..." She closed her eyes against the humiliation. She'd told Cal she loved him the same night he'd stolen the information. But she'd never told Cain or Jonathon, even during the debriefing when she discovered the files had been compromised.

"I told Cain," Cal said quietly. "When I started working

for Labyrinth, he insisted on full disclosure. Remember, our relationship was business."

"And Cain's banking on the fact that Jason will keep you safe because I loved you?"

Neither mentioned the fact she used the past tense. Past or present, it didn't matter.

"That's why Jason found me at the bar. He'd heard about our affair through channels," Cal admitted. "I confirmed it."

"Channels?"

"Either Cain or Mercer, I imagine."

"God, you're all a piece of work," she retorted, then shoved a hand through her hair, pushing the locks away from her face with frustration. "For a moment I'd thought you'd changed. That I could trust you."

"Nothing has changed, don't ever forget it," Cal snapped out. "I'm the man who slept with you to have access to your security. I accessed top secret information on the computer and traded it with another country for intelligence on a terrorist sect in London."

Humiliation crept up her spine. She stiffened against it.

"You figured it out, told your boss. My government agreed to an equal exchange of our technology and my hands were slapped. A year later, I'm an operative for the same government I stole from. It's how it works. You were a tool, Julia. That's all."

Her sharp intake of breath told him he'd drawn blood. And lots of it. But Cal was beyond caring. His own needs raged within him. Cain had insisted on full disclosure because at the time, Julia had been Cal's weakness. His Achilles' heel.

"It's a fact Jason still cares for you. The bar fight confirmed that."

"That still doesn't answer one question."

Cal turned his back on her and walked through the living room into the small galley kitchen. "Drop it."

"Not on your life," she replied, following him. "Jason made sure I sought help from you. It always bothered me. You betrayed me once, why would you be the one he trusted to protect me?"

"I'll have to remember to ask him why when I see him."

"You already know why. But for some reason, you aren't telling me," she argued.

Love happened, damn it. Somewhere after the jungle and before the bar fight he fell in love with Julia. When Jason confronted him, Cal had been hurting. Jason saw it immediately.

Decency and desire warred within him, breaking through his control. It pierced the surface, tightened his features.

He stepped in, putting them hip to hip, chest to chest, her back against the refrigerator. Confusion flashed across her face, then God help him, desire ignited the amber in her eyes.

He grabbed her wrists in one hand and locked them against the door above her head. His slid his free hand behind her neck, cupped its nape and brought her up close until they were nose to nose. His hips ground against hers, making sure she understood just how much he wanted her.

Hard and hot, his mouth devoured hers, his hunger erupting into a rampage of need. He let her hands go, hoping deep down, she'd fight him.

"Stop me now, Julia. Because if you don't I'll take more than your body. I'll take your pride, your love. I'll take your bloody soul before I'm done this time," he threatened. *And give you mine,* he vowed silently. "Then I'll walk away. And I won't look back."

Instead, she gripped his shoulders and curved into his heat.

He growled, biting her bottom lip until she opened her mouth.

Without warning, her sweetness poured through him,

morphing his cravings into a fit of hunger. Old memories of her raced through his mind. Naked pictures of them tangled in bed. Her silky skin, hot beneath his hands, trembling beneath his mouth.

Swift and ugly, his desire turned on him. It gained momentum, an avalanche of need that swept his feet out from under him, tumbling him into a dark abyss.

Desperate, he fitted his mouth tight and gathered her close, his arms locked around her in a bloody battle for restraint.

Delicate hands moved to his back stroking and soothing, even as he plunged and pillaged.

Then he tasted the salt of her tears.

He pulled back. His heart raced, his breath came in long, ragged gulps of air. Tears streaked her cheeks, ran down to her jaw.

He stole the information, turned her away from him so she couldn't be used as a tool for revenge. Everything in the past, he'd done for her. To keep her alive.

This he'd done for himself. To escape his demons.

He ran a thumb over her lips, felt the soft kiss she left on his skin.

Her lips were swollen, nearly bruised. Her gaze solemn and God help him, full of trust.

He dug deep for the strength to shatter that trust.

"You really have no pride, do you, Julia?"

The verbal slap snapped her head back, drained the color from her face.

"You bastard," she said after a moment, struggling to keep her voice even. For all her height, her frame was delicate, but not fragile. "And you got what you wanted, Cal. I'll stay with Esteban. Anything is better than sharing the same air with you."

The strength of spirit, her stubbornness rose against him. Almost overpowering him.

He'd forgotten.

Until now.

Pride for her filled his chest, but it was the self-loathing that filled his heart—that nearly brought him to his knees.

"We've wasted enough time." He stepped back, sickened with self-disgust. "I'll give you five minutes to get ready. We have to meet Renalto."

"I don't need five minutes." Julia's breath backed up in her chest, squeezed her heart until it bled out.

And when this is done, I won't need you, she vowed silently.

Chapter Nine

The hangar predated World War I. Its sides more rust than steel, its gaps more holes than crevices.

But the building did its job. It was far enough from the airport traffic to keep under the radar, but sturdy enough to house an occasional plane.

Renalto studied the plane that stood center stage. A four-seater Piper Comanche with enough rust and dents to put the old hangar to shame.

In his mind, he placed the hangar into the black-and-white backdrop of an old television show.

For the millionth time, he cursed himself for choosing the law, rather than the life of a performer.

After all, hadn't he proven he was the consummate actor? He had the looks of the aristocrat with his long, lean bones and sharpened features. With eyes of onyx, that enticed many señoritas into his bed.

It took talent to walk the line between the lawful and the illicit, to manipulate the key players in life's little dramas.

Leopold had been one of those people, a little voice whispered from the back of his mind.

Renalto swore. Even Leopold had been driven by greed, he argued silently. The old man had known the dangers, had taken the payment offered.

He also had died, leaving a family of five with little more than the clothes on their backs.

Uncomfortable with the thought, Renalto pushed it away. And with it, the small splinter of guilt wedged between his shoulder blades.

"This is our transportation?"

Renalto turned, grateful for the distraction. "It was the best I could do, *amigo*," he said.

He waited until Cal crossed to the plane before he added, "You want something faster? We can always use your Learjet."

Julia stepped up from behind Cal and blinked in surprise. "You have a jet?"

"A small one. Yes." He frowned hard at Renalto. "Not that it matters."

"Oh, it matters," Julia cut in.

"I've made good investments over the years, Julia. Nothing more." Cal walked over to the plane in three quick strides. "And I like planes. Although this one is a little outdated for my taste."

"When was it built?" she asked, curious now.

"Mid-nineteen-fifties," Renalto answered. Cal had eased up into the cockpit for a closer look at the instruments.

"It looks like it will fall out of the sky the minute it hits a crosswind," Cal commented.

"It has heart." Renalto deliberately paused and wiggled his eyebrows to Julia. "Trust me."

Charmed, Julia grinned. "Is this a private hangar?" She noted the scrap metal and engine parts scattered in the far corners.

"Yes," Renalto answered. "But we don't have to worry about the owner."

Julia noted the cot against the back wall. "Are you staying here, Renalto?"

"Yes." Renalto followed her line of sight. "Since my place was destroyed."

"Who is the owner?" Cal asked. The words held just

enough arrogance to give Julia the impression that Cal knew the answer.

"Me." Renalto grinned and slapped Cal on the shoulder. "It always pays to have alternative transportation." He nodded to the taxi just beyond the hangar's opening. "Especially when your other vehicle is rendered practically useless."

"I'll buy you another," Cal stated.

Obviously Cal decided not to hide his bank account now that his Learjet had been outed, Julia mused.

"Did Jason know about your plane?" she asked, curious as to how close Renalto was to her ex.

"No," Renalto stated. For the first time since she'd met him, Renalto's voice took a hard tone. His features slanted into sharp edges. "The only reason *you* do, is because I have a score to settle with Delgado."

CALVIN PROPPED HIS SHOULDER AGAINST the bedroom door. The early morning moisture from the jungle still clung to his clothes.

An hour past dawn brought slices of morning light through the cracks of the curtains. Somewhere during the heat of the night, Julia shoved off the comforter, leaving it a mangled mess at her feet. She slept on her stomach, her backside up, her head buried under the pillow. That, Cal thought, amused, hadn't changed.

Many times in the past, he'd run his hand over the curve of her backside, slowly bringing her awake when his fingers wandered into the sweet spots between.

Her T-shirt had ridden up her back sometime during the night, leaving the feminine line of her spine almost entirely exposed. The silky skin, flushed in a sleepy pink hue, tempted him to rediscover what he'd walked away from so long ago.

Desire reared, biting at the back of his spine. Its sharp

teeth gnawing, forcing Cal to straighten from the door. Forcing himself to remember why he'd walked away in the first place.

Julia was just another casualty of war.

And Calvin understood war. He'd spent a short stint in the midst of the desert conflict overseas, returning with a few medals pinned over the scars he earned. The recognition bought him a large chunk of time in the jungle. His job was neutralizing the low-level humans who worked for Cristo Delgado, Esteban Alvarez and many more of the same. Killing them, he corrected silently. Years of it.

It didn't matter anymore that these men murdered innocent children, whole families, including pregnant women. He'd been drowning in his own immorality. Until Julia.

When Cal had started dating her, it had been a casual thought. To take care of a serious attraction. What he didn't expect was to fall in love.

Or that he'd make her a contracted target for Delgado's revenge.

Left no choice, Cal walked away.

And when she'd followed him, he'd hurt her.

Better hurt than dead, Jon Mercer reasoned with him at the time.

Julia turned over, her eyes blinked open. Shadows darkened the delicate skin beneath her eyes.

For a moment, she'd forgotten their circumstance. Her smile was warm and lazy and inviting. Oxygen caught in his chest, making it tight. Then slowly reality blossomed and dimmed the amber of her eyes, tightened the soft features into sharp edges.

"What time is it?" she asked, her tone flat.

"Just after eight," he said, suddenly wanting the smile back, the invitation there. He clenched his jaw. "I'm getting ready to make some eggs, toast and coffee. So if you want, you have time to take a shower."

"All right." She stretched her arms above her head, then froze when his eyes drifted over her. Slowly, her arms returned to her sides. "When do we contact Alvarez?"

"In about two hours," Cal replied, with a briskness he didn't feel. "After, I'm to meet Renalto at the airport so we can take off."

"You seem pretty sure Alvarez will agree to your terms."

"I am sure." Cal tried to keep his gaze neutral and off her bare shoulders, the curve of her neck. "I've negotiated these kind of deals before."

"Is that what you did when you were with MI6?" she asked.

"Among other things."

"What other things?"

"Ugly things. With nasty people," he mused grimly. "Years of it."

Slowly, she slid her legs across the bed and sat up. "I'll accept that I have to stay behind on this leg of the trip. If you promise me to come back—alive."

She tried to smile, tried to make light of her request. But the smile didn't quite mask the concern that haunted her eyes.

"Any promise I make would be a lie. And we both know it."

"Even if it's a lie, Cal, promise me," she insisted.

"I can't," he said softly. "Not this time, Julia."

He fought the impulse to gather her close, hold her tight. To promise her anything to make them both feel better.

"Take a shower," he ordered, his tone grim but determined. "I'll see to breakfast."

JULIA STEPPED OUT OF THE RENTED Hummer and braced her legs to keep them from buckling. The vehicle had hit every jut and groove on the two-track road, setting her teeth on edge, leaving her neck muscles aching.

The humidity had solidified with the noon sun's heat. Thick and wet, it coated her skin like a soggy wool blanket.

Logic clashed against loyalty. Jason's son's life was at stake, but Julia had promised Jason she would not tell Calvin about the boy. Jason said he knew too much about Cal to trust him.

Julia couldn't help believe that Jason was wrong. That Calvin would find a way to save Jason's son if he knew of his existence.

Esteban walked from a nearby building and clasped both of her hands in his. "Ms. Cutting, I have decided to take Calvin up on his offer."

"So it seems," she replied, then tugged at his hold. "And considering the circumstances, Julia seems more appropriate."

"Julia." He inclined his head, his eyes glinting with amusement. But Esteban didn't release her.

"I think first names are appropriate considering," Tessa added and stepped forward. Her outstretched hand forced Esteban to let Julia go. "Good morning, Julia."

"Tessa." Dressed in a cool, white, sleeveless blouse and sea-foam-green skirt, the woman appeared as if she was on a casual stroll down New York's Fifth Avenue.

Julia glanced down at her own lightweight beige cotton pants, white tank top under a moss-green cotton shirt and a darker blue bandana tied around her neck.

Not the height of fashion, but Cal insisted when she donned her new pair of hiking boots.

"If the helicopter is shot down, you'd better be dressed for it," he'd warned.

"I am looking forward to the company of another woman," Tessa added lightly, obviously seeing Julia's swift assessment.

"Thank you." Julia smiled and realized under different circumstances, she could have been friends with Tessa.

"Do you have luggage?"

"Right here," Cal announced from behind the group. He handed the small black overnight bag to Esteban.

"The helicopter is already being prepared." The drug dealer nodded to the tarmac where a brand-new Black Hawk helicopter sat.

"Nice ride. Nicer upgrades," Cal commented, noting the high-back chairs and leather interior. "Hard to come by. Most governments aren't good sharers when it comes to this kind of transportation."

"I have friends who have a few of these, but many more vices. It is a good trade," Esteban replied matter-of-factly. "We'll take it out to my private retreat. It's about an hour's distance from here."

The four started toward the helicopter.

"You'll be annoyed, Cal. But we'll be flying over Cristo's villa."

"Coincidence?" Cal asked.

"Certainly not." Esteban tsked, then patted the breast pocket of his navy striped tailored suit. He brought out a long, thin cigarette and lit it. "It was more…convenient… when our business dealings were more interlocked."

"How many business dealings do you have with Delgado now?"

"None," Esteban admitted.

"When was the last time you visited his villa, Alvarez?" Cal asked.

"Two weeks ago for dinner." The other man's gaze sharpened, even as his features relaxed, and his mouth slid into an easy smile. He took another drag of his cigarette and then tossed it to the cement. "It's best to keep up appearances, don't you think, Mr. West?"

"Or your enemies close," Cal commented, then stopped several feet away from the helicopter.

He turned to Julia. "I'll be back in a few days."

When she said nothing, he stepped close and tipped her chin up until their faces were mere inches apart.

The breath caught in her chest. He will come back, she told herself. With Jason. Then they'll rescue Argus together.

Cal's gaze skimmed her features, locked on to her eyes. "Don't worry, Julia, I'll get Jason back."

"I'm worried about both of you, Cal. Just make sure you come back, too." She didn't close the distance between them. The urge to kiss him goodbye vibrated through her, but she refused to give in to it.

The pilot—a small, slim man with a pointed goatee and saggy blue eyes—approached the group. "Señor Alvarez, we are ready."

"Very well, Malachi. See to Ms. Cutting's valise, please."

"Here." Cal handed over the bag to the pilot, but his gaze stayed on Julia.

Esteban gave Julia a short bow. "After you."

"Thank you." She turned on her heel and took a step. Suddenly, Cal grabbed her arm.

"Bloody hell," he muttered. Then tugged her into his arms, brought her lips beneath his.

Her world blurred into the heat waves of the tarmac, the heat of his mouth on hers.

She parted her lips, wanting more, needing more, hoping the reassurance she sought could be found in the depth of his kiss.

All too soon, he pulled back, leaving her with little more comfort than she had that morning.

His thumb stroked her chin, then nudged it up. "Stay out of trouble," he murmured against her forehead.

"Oh, my." Tessa cleared her throat. "I think now we're ready to go."

Cal released Julia and stepped away. "I'll see you soon."

With that, he started back toward the Hummer.

"Your Calvin West must either be a very smart man or a very stupid one," Esteban remarked, his tone loud enough to be heard over the chopper blades. "He's taking one hell of a chance leaving you with me."

Julia glanced at Tessa, then back at Esteban. "I don't think he takes chances. I think he understood the situation that we're in and adapted."

"But you are not pleased," Tessa inserted. "Because his decision left both of the men you care about in danger and out of your reach. Did it not?"

Julia didn't say anything. That had been the problem all along. While she'd known Jason most of her life, dated him through college and then married him, life had turned them into strangers, but still, she cared for him deeply.

Something she was sure Cal didn't understand.

"Don't judge West too harshly, Julia," Esteban commented.

The rush of the wind from the helicopter blades kicked up the dust and grit from the tarmac, sent the tips of the nearby trees swaying.

Esteban took her elbow and helped first her, then Tessa into the helicopter.

Both women placed the headsets over their ears. "He'll be fine, Julia," Tessa said, once they'd both settled in. "Both he and your ex-husband are very good at what they do. They'll be in and out before Cristo is aware of what hit him."

Julia nodded, but the knots in her stomach tightened. What if they couldn't go back? Cristo would certainly double his security once Cal breached his compound.

Julia realized the huge miscalculation she made. One that put a boy's life more at stake.

"You'll have another chance with him," Tessa added, understanding. "Just make the next kiss better than the last."

"I think I will," Julia agreed, deciding. With urgent fingers, she unsnapped her safety belt. "Esteban, I will be right back."

CALVIN WATCHED THE THREE OF THEM get into the helicopter. Two bodyguards followed, each the size of human tanks. But it was Malachi who drew his attention.

Wiry and thin, the pilot flicked a cigarette nervously while he waited for Alvarez to board. Then every so often, the man's gaze darted to the jungle's edge and back again.

The hairs stood at the back of Cal's scalp. It could be he was overreacting. After all, Cal admitted silently, he wasn't happy about letting Julia out of his sight.

But taking her into the jungle with him and Renalto would be unnecessarily exposing her to danger.

Cal slid into the Hummer's driver seat and turned the ignition. The air-conditioner hit him full in the face, but did little to relieve the heat from Julia's kiss.

Cal glanced in the rearview mirror for one last reassuring look and noted the pilot's position outside the belly of the helicopter.

Suddenly, Julia jumped from the opposite door, escaping the pilot's notice.

She started running toward the Hummer.

"Bloody hell." Cal shoved the Hummer door open again.

Malachi's cigarette slipped from his fingers and fell to the tarmac.

Warning whispered across the base of Cal's neck. His eyes narrowed on the pilot. Malachi reached for the butt, but rather than just pick it up, the man looked around, then flipped a latch on the belly of the copter.

It was then the pilot noticed Julia running across the tarmac.

The helicopter's engine sputtered.

Cal pulled his pistol out of his shoulder holster, threw the Hummer in Reverse and hit the gas.

GUNFIRE BURST FROM THE JUNGLE, peppering the airfield, pinging off the helicopter's tail and rotor.

Esteban jumped from the helicopter, machine gun in hand. "The jungle!" He strafed the jungle's edge with a burst from his gun.

Julia scanned the treeline as she ran toward the Hummer. "They are shooting from the jungle," she screamed the warning.

Two guards scrambled out of the helicopter behind Esteban and fired their machine guns into the dense foliage.

Cal swerved back, hit the brakes. The Hummer spun one hundred and eighty degrees until it stopped between Julia and the crossfire. He hit the button, lowering the window. "Get in," Cal ordered.

He watched, his pistol raised. A body appeared, scrambling for cover behind a tree. Cal fired. The man screamed and fell to the ground.

"If we stay, we'll be boxed in," Cal acknowledged. He glanced back toward the hangar, saw Renalto dive back through the side door. A barrage of bullets struck the door moments later.

No help there.

Cal hit the gas. The Hummer raced across the tarmac toward the jungle.

"What are you doing?" Julia screamed.

"We're surrounded by a small army of guerillas from the

looks of it. But whoever they are, they don't want us dead. Otherwise we would be already. The field is too open for them to charge us for a while."

"Esteban's men can't hold them off much longer," Julia urged.

"Then we get lost in the jungle."

Gunfire exploded from behind them, the tires gave out from underneath them.

"Hold on!" Cal jerked the wheel, putting the car into a full spin.

"What's the backup plan?" Julia asked after the Hummer came to a stop.

"We use some of the toys Renalto left in the back of the car for cover and head into the jungle."

"The same jungle where the bullets are coming from?"

Cal nodded toward the open airstrip toward the hangars. "I can get us lost in the jungle. Out there on the tarmac we're sitting ducks."

Chapter Ten

"Did you see West race back to the Cutter woman? Some-how the pilot gave himself away." Carlos spat at the ground, revealing a row of decaying, brown teeth. "Considering how much it cost us to buy him off—"

Without warning, an explosion hit the ground twenty feet away, sending two of Solaris's men flying through the air.

Carlos swore and peered through the brush. Calvin and Julia abandoned the Hummer at the edge of the rainforest and slipped between the trees on foot.

"Grenades! Take cover!" Solaris yelled as another went off nearby. The blast knocked Solaris off his feet. He shook his head and looked up, only to see Carlos's eyes wide open, a gaping hole of bone and muscle in his chest.

"Find West and the woman. Bring them to me," Solaris yelled. But when he turned around, he realized his men had scattered.

"ARE YOU OUT OF YOUR MIND?" Julia shouted, letting her anger take over, rather than dealing with the fear and relief that made her legs jelly. "What were you thinking? Taking on an army of men?"

"Maybe that it's my job. That I've been trained to take down terrorists and guerillas. And that you haven't. Yet you run across a bloody airstrip after me. No guns, no protection. I'll ask why after I cool down a bit."

"It's no longer important. I—"

"No longer important?" He pulled her up until they were eye to eye. "If you value your life, you won't say another word for the next five minutes."

When he released her, Julia stumbled back. It was then she noticed the dead bodies. Some dressed in fatigues, others in street clothes or a combination of both. "These were Delgado's men?"

"Or hired locals," Cal confirmed. "Although I'd be hard-pressed to believe that Cristo would want to hire amateurs." Cal scanned the trees. "Even if we searched the jungle, the dead won't tell us who hired them. And anyone else is long gone now."

He adjusted the pack he retrieved from the back of the Hummer. Kept the assault rifle in his hand. "We should have enough to get us through the next few days."

"Cristo must be getting impatient," Julia said. "He must want us pretty bad."

"Not me. You."

"That's reassuring."

"Cristo would consider it a bonus if Esteban turned up dead." Cal hacked through the jungle's thick undergrowth with a machete. "Me, too."

The Black Hawk roared in the distance. Julia placed her hand over her eyebrows to block the sun. Esteban's helicopter skimmed the treetops, heading east. "Looks like Esteban and Tessa escaped."

"They won't get very far with most of their fuel left on the tarmac."

"Do you think Esteban was behind the attack?"

"No," Cal replied honestly. "He has too much to lose and Tessa is too smart to let him lose it."

"So, Delgado would have kept me alive," she wondered out loud. "And Tessa? If they'd gotten their hands on her?"

"She'd have been pleading to die soon enough."

Julia understood the same would be said for her if Delgado captured her and found out she didn't have the MONGREL.

"Where are we going?"

"Now that's a question, isn't it?" he said. "I saw the pilot sabotage the helicopter. If Delgado paid off Esteban's pilot, there is no way of knowing who else in his household has been paid off. So it looks like you got what you wanted. You're coming with me and we're going to help Jason escape. That's the only way we're going to get the hell out of this situation."

Birds squawked, setting the trees rustling, the monkeys scurrying. Julia glanced up, caught the flash of neon green and yellow.

"Yucatan," Cal commented. "They're good at keeping the snakes at a marginal capacity."

"That's comforting," Julia muttered, ignoring a foot-long lizard that skittered across her path.

"There's a road about five hundred yards west of this clearing. We'll follow the edge. We need to make about ten miles before dusk, which is a good clip."

"Won't we be seen?"

"We'll have enough warning to take cover in the trees. It's safer than hitting a trap set near someone's coca or marijuana crop."

"Trap?"

"Trip wires. Mines. Pits with snakes."

"Aren't they worried about their own people getting injured or killed?"

"The locals know where they all are, trust me. But even if they don't, they are willing to take their chances. The people here get paid a lot of money to work for the cartels. They take the risk and they don't use the merchandise. Both might get them killed. When they can't do the work, they send in their children."

"Children?" Nausea swirled in Julia's belly as she thought of some of the children racing along the streets. "They grow up fast around here, don't they?"

"Pretty much like the poorest parts of the cities in the States or in Britain. Children are left no choice sometimes."

Julia heard the underlining hardness in Cal's voice and understood where the comment came from.

He had spent the first ten years of his life on the streets of London. Fifteen and pregnant, his mother was disowned by blue-blood parents. But when Cal was ten, Maureen West took pity on her friend's daughter and hired her as an upstairs maid. His mother spent the next couple years with the West family and soon fell in love with their oldest son, Henry West.

General Sir Henry West was recently retired from the Chief of General staff, commander of the British Army. He adopted Calvin soon after the marriage and Julia suspected Cal's admiration for his father led him to a life with the government.

"How are your parents?"

"I haven't actually seen them in a long time." Cal swept a branch away from the side before it could hit Julia in the face. "I imagine retirement is agreeing with them."

When he didn't elaborate, she wasn't surprised. That side of him he kept closely guarded. It was the one thing they had in common.

Chapter Eleven

The jungle canopy hung low, blocking most of the late-afternoon sun but did little to diminish its potency. The rays pierced the thick undergrowth giving light to their path, while its strength pushed the temperature to over one hundred degrees.

Julia took off her bandana and wiped her forehead.

"We only have a little more daylight left." Cal's comment broke through their silence. He pointed north. "Storm clouds will be rolling in soon, too."

He held out a protein bar he wrestled from his pocket. "Are you hungry?"

"No." Julia rolled her shoulders, but didn't slow down. "How long do we have to travel tomorrow before we reach Jason?"

"Don't expect the Jason you know waiting for you with open arms, Julia." Calvin handed her the canteen. "He may be compromised."

"By compromised, you mean tortured. Right?" Julia sighed and swallowed some water.

"There's a good chance the man we rescue won't be a man at all. The tactics used on the cartel enemies are inhuman. Worse, Delgado and his men take pleasure from inflicting pain. It deters others from trying to cross them."

"They won't go too far, Cal. Not without the MONGREL,"

she argued. "Besides, I've checked all the intelligence on the case. There is no indication that Jason has been compromised."

"Don't fool yourself. They've tortured him, they're just not ready to advertise it," Cal warned. "And if they haven't, there's a good possibility he's switched sides."

"Treason isn't his style." But doubt nudged her. Determined, Julia forced it back and changed the subject. "How long have you known Jason?"

"A few years," Cal answered. "Most of the agents I've known have specific talents. Jason is no different. He's got a talent for winning confidences. A valuable commodity in our business."

"What do you mean?"

"Jason can interrogate any prisoner, make them feel like he's on their side and within hours, have them sharing crucial information." Cal lifted a negligent shoulder. "I've needed his talents every so often."

"He'd have made a brilliant lawyer," Julia acknowledged. "And the favor? You mentioned that among other things, Jason saved your life. What other things?"

Cal sighed. "For years, Jason had worked on breaking Delgado's shipping lines. Finally, a year ago he managed to extradite one of Delgado's lieutenants. A man by the name of Vicente Padrino who had firsthand knowledge of Delgado's business."

"A year ago?" Julia frowned. "That's when you and I met."

"Yes," Cal admitted. "During that time, Jordan Beck and I traced the smuggling of a small nuclear bomb into the United States."

"I remember," she said. "It was set to go off in Washington, D.C., on Christmas day, but you, Jordan and Regina disarmed it just in time."

"We almost didn't, actually," Cal corrected. "We were in

the last twenty-four hours and I needed information regarding the people involved with the nuclear bomb. Padrino turned out to be that link."

"So Jason helped you out."

"Jason got the information, but not without making a deal," Cal explained. "Padrino negotiated his release for the information."

Julia guessed the rest. "He headed straight back to South America."

"The bloody idiot figured he could talk his way back into Delgado's good graces. Two weeks later, locals found Padrino's mutilated body beside a road. Delgado just tossed him out the car door when they were through with their fun."

"And Jason?"

"We saved the day finding and then disarming two bombs. One in London, the other in Washington, D.C., but not before Jason's Delgado indictments fell apart."

"How did he take it?"

"Not well," Cal admitted. "Which could have led to Jason's defection a few weeks ago. The Caracas airport tapes show him getting off the plane. He flew under an alias, walked out of the airport and disappeared. No contact. A few weeks later, Renalto found out Jason had been taken by Delgado."

Or he wanted his son, she thought. "That's not Jason," Julia said instead. "If he's anything, he is logical, analytical but not impulsive."

"Except when he left you and joined the DEA. That certainly was impulsive."

"Even that he planned for a long time. He just kept the information to himself." Julia thought about it for a moment. "No, he went into Delgado's compound with a backup plan. The MONGREL was his collateral."

"Possibly." But Cal understood that if he'd been in Jason's

spot, he'd move hell and earth to make sure she remained safe from the likes of Delgado.

"You said Jason divorced you. What did you mean?"

"Our marriage had never been anything more than a few weeks together here and there over the years. Eventually, we only shared phone calls. Finally, the phone calls just stopped," Julia answered. "Soon after I started working for Jon Mercer. He was Labyrinth's director at the time. When his personal assistant was arrested for treason, I stepped in and ultimately took her job."

"I remember hearing about that. Kate MacAlister D'Amato discovered the leak, didn't she?"

Julia nodded. "At the time, she was hiding out with her husband, Roman."

"And now you're chasing after Jason."

"Not entirely, Cal," she said, getting the nerve to tell him the truth.

He didn't give her a chance. He was determined to figure out her relationship with her ex-husband. "When was the last time you talked to Jason?"

"When he called me about your favor. That was a month ago."

"Before that?"

"Not seriously since the divorce," Julia admitted, annoyed. "This is starting to sound like an interrogation, Cal."

Jealousy nipped at his heels. But he was smart enough to know it wasn't the driving force behind the questions.

Julia's safety was foremost. He couldn't figure out why Jason sent her into this mess in the first place when he could have contacted Cal directly.

"So you're saying after several years of no communication, Jason shows up on your doorstep?"

"Not from out of nowhere," she explained. His pace picked up with his anger. Julia kept her eyes on the ground, watched her footing. "From Colombia. Or at least that's what he told me. I have no reason to think he lied."

"Weren't you surprised?"

"At seeing him?" She thought for a moment. "Not really. There was a lot left unfinished between us. Maybe I thought it would eventually have to be resolved."

"When did you last see him, Julia?"

"Before this?"

Cal nodded.

"Once at the beach on Chesapeake Bay." For a time after her breakup with Cal, Julia found solace during long walks on the beach. "It was the first time that I noticed Jason had truly changed."

"How?"

"He'd been swimming in the surf when he noticed me, he called my name," she remembered. "He'd grown leaner, but not in a good way. His arms and stomach showed scars from recent wounds."

Julia used to check the scars on Cal's body, looking for any fresh ones when he got back from assignments.

"He'd even gotten a few tattoos. One on his chest. A peacock." The Jason she'd married would have never considered a tattoo. Believed people eventually regretted their impulse to mark their body. But she realized later, he'd done it for other reasons.

In Greek mythology, Argus was Hera's giant who had a hundred eyes. Eventually, Hermes killed him. Heartbroken, she transferred Argus's eyes to the tail of a peacock.

Jason tattooed the peacock over his heart.

"We didn't say much," Julia continued. "Some small talk and a quick goodbye. He seemed concerned about me, though. He hadn't showed me much attention in a long while."

"Why?"

"I told you, we didn't have a typical marriage." She swiped at a bug on her cheek. "Jason's father and my father were, at one time, legal partners. Jason and I grew up together. Our lives had been planned from the beginning. Only the best nannies, the best private schools, then Ivy League colleges. I don't think either of us questioned it because we'd always had each other. For most of my life, Jason was my best friend. Both of us following in our fathers' footsteps, both of us being groomed as corporate lawyers."

"So, naturally you married."

"There wasn't anything natural about it, actually. We were too much alike, too much like siblings. But neither of us knew how to tell our parents. Or maybe we just hoped we were wrong, that a love born from friendship would turn into something more…" Unable to find an answer, she shrugged. "Just something more, I guess.

"After graduating from law school, we married. The perfect society-column marriage. Theodore Marsh's son and Maxwell Cutting's daughter."

Suddenly restless, she picked up her pace until she was next to Cal. "We honeymooned for three weeks in the Caribbean. We'd become more strangers than friends by that time because of the pressure of the wedding, our new careers. The trip was a disaster and it was the best part of the marriage. Six months later, he joined the DEA and disappeared from my life." But not before she understood that he'd lumped her with his parents and their shallow circle of friends—that he had chosen a life with the DEA to get away from all of them.

But then the truth always did hurt. And the truth was Jason had been right.

"His father was disgusted with the way Jason threw away a brilliant career so he disowned him."

"And your parents?"

"Since I failed in making my marriage work, I'm treated

with a tolerable indifference. The ice defrosted a bit once I followed Jon Mercer to the White House," Julia admitted. What she didn't admit, couldn't admit, was how she'd learned to deal with the loneliness. Or how they'd turned her into a product of their environment. The perfectly coiffed, polished and predictable daughter.

"I bet you made good bragging rights at the dinner table."

"Something like that. Although I was rarely invited to those dinner parties."

Calvin felt her retreat, recognized it for what it was. Self-defense. Something he understood.

From the moment he'd met Julia at the Oval Office, he'd been attracted. It had been his first meeting with President Mercer.

But it wasn't until he ran into her, literally, during a jog that he'd made his move.

A heavy mist settled into the early-evening air, turned it thick with humidity. Warm drops of water pelted the leaves around them.

"The rain's coming. We'll stop here until morning."

Cal's voice caught her off guard. She stopped and took in her surroundings.

He'd found a small hill, its base dense with foliage.

"Where?"

Calvin shook some branches free from the hillside. Just beyond, Julia saw the opening of a small cave.

"How did you know this was here?"

"I hid out here for a month one time, many years ago. Almost ten now. I'd been dodging Delgado's men for a week," he said, careful not to break any vines, trample the under-growth. "Solaris tracked me to the river. Jason shot Solaris and helped me escape. I was shot up pretty bad so he brought me here. He left me with supplies and first aid, and then managed to get word back to my government to come and get me."

"I didn't realize," Julia responded. "You can't tell me that the same man who saved your life is trying to betray our government."

"That was over ten years ago. A lot of things can happen to a person over a decade."

"Is that why you used me, Cal? Did working for the government change you that much?"

"Yes," he lied, but this time the word lay bitterly against his tongue. "Give me a minute to check out the cave, then follow me in."

He snapped a couple of glow sticks and handed her one. "I want to make sure it's not being used as a home for any of the animals around here."

Julia stood outside and kept her eyes peeled for any of Cristo's men.

After waiting two minutes, she went down on her knees and crawled into the hole.

Once in the entrance, the cave's ceiling heightened another couple of feet, making it possible for her to stand almost straight.

It smelled of fresh vegetation and strong soil. Comforting in a strange way. She tossed the glow stick next to his on the ground.

"No fires," Cal advised. This time he handed her the protein bar. "Eat this. You need to keep up your strength."

Julia sat cross-legged on the ground and tore open the package. "What is your plan once we reach Delgado's?"

"I have a friend who lives only a short distance from Delgado's compound."

"If he lives that close are you sure he's a friend?" she countered. She took a bite of the bar, ignored the chalky, dry taste. "How long has it been since you've seen him?"

"Last year," Cal answered after a long pause. "I was here on a fact-gathering mission."

"What kind of facts?"

Cal considered not telling her for a moment. Maybe he was tired of the subterfuge or just simply tired.

"I was sent in to kidnap Argus Delgado," Cal replied, a grim line to his face.

"Cristo's son?" Fear trickled down Julia's back. "Why?"

"If Cristo had lost his son, then it would have put his whole organization into turmoil. His competitors, his lieutenants would have been vying for control of his empire. It's no secret that Cristo is grooming Argus to take over everything. His devotion to the boy is his one Achilles' heel."

"And after you kidnapped him?" Julia finished her bar and wiped her hands on her pants. "What would have happened to him then?"

"He would have been placed in a government protection program probably."

"Against his will?"

"Most likely."

"And his mother?"

"She's Delgado's wife first. Argus's mother second," Cal replied. "She's also an addict. No matter how much she loves her son, she won't leave her supply."

"And if he loved his parents?"

"His wants wouldn't be taken into consideration. He's no more than a pawn as far as we were concerned."

"You being Labyrinth," she said dully. "So why didn't you kidnap him?"

"Cain MacAlister," Cal said. "He suspected a leak. He scrubbed the operation. A week later, Cristo put a price on my head."

"Who did Cain suspect of leaking the information?" she asked, but already knew the answer.

"Jason."

Chapter Twelve

The cave chilled with the night air, but the dampness, the strong scents of jungle clung to its walls.

Cal buried one of the glow sticks beneath the dirt, giving the cave a denser, almost eerie mood.

It took a while for her eyes to adjust, but soon shadows shifted into vague, but decipherable patterns.

Cal had taken off his shoes but otherwise had stayed fully dressed like she had. He laid a thin silver blanket on the ground barely big enough to hold his frame.

"Are we sharing?" she asked.

"That's the idea." When she hesitated, he sighed. "It's going to be a long day tomorrow, Julia. I suggest you get some sleep." He stretched out on the blanket and closed his eyes.

"What are you planning for tomorrow?" Nerves pricked under her skin. During their time together, they had never just slept together and she wasn't quite sure how she felt about doing it now.

Cal gave her a curt nod. "We're going to get in touch with a friend of mine."

"Another Renalto?" she questioned, her eyebrow raised.

"Not quite," he answered, his tone dry, but with a hint of humor.

"Cal," she said. "You said earlier that most operatives have their special talents. What did you mean?"

"Exactly that. Jordan Beck was the man of disguises, Roman D'Amato was security. Cain is known as a strategist. And his brother, Ian, a hunter. The man could track a snake across a hundred miles of rocks."

"And you, Cal? What are you known for?"

"I neutralized situations before they got out of hand."

"You neutralized situations," she repeated. "Meaning?"

"They brought me in when the regular channels didn't provide results," Cal stated. "A diplomat of sorts."

"That's vague," she commented, her tone edged with annoyance.

Cal opened his eyes. It was getting harder and harder to keep up the lies. Harder and harder to keep an emotional distance.

"Look, Julia. What I do is top secret. I could tell you about my mission, but then I'd have to kill you," he explained. He swiped a hand over his face, rubbed the whiskers on his cheek. "I'm too tired to do either."

"Very funny."

"What's funny is that we've slept together countless times, but for some reason you can't bring yourself to lie next to me."

"That's not it—"

"If I promise not to attack you, will you lie down so we both can get some sleep?"

Embarrassed, Julia realized Cal was right. After all, they were both adults. They could manage one night together, sleeping.

She settled next to him, immediately relaxing against the warmth of his side.

The rain was coming down in torrents. For a moment Julia stilled and listened.

Shivers rifled through her, shuddered into him. Startled, she shifted to put some distance between them. Her chest brushed up against his side, she felt his breath soft against her cheek, the scrape of his teeth against her earlobe.

His arms tightened on her and without warning, he rolled her onto her back, catching her between the hard earth and the harder planes of his body. Using one elbow to hold his weight, he caressed her cheek with his free hand. "Julia—"

"Shh." She didn't want him to stop—understood this would be for one night. Understood that she needed the solace, the warmth of his touch, then walk away, her heart whole.

Julia turned her head until her lips pressed against the palm of his hand.

When his mouth covered hers, he did so slowly, as if he was savoring the soft, feminine taste of her.

She looked from underneath her lashes, saw his eyes open, the black heat piercing the semidarkness between them. Her body trembled.

With a groan, his kiss changed. He slanted his mouth over hers, taking, coaxing, feasting.

Igniting a heat inside her that smoked, swirled then burst into a fever of desire that threatened to consume her.

Wanting to touch her, needing to, he rolled onto his back, taking her with him until she laid sprawled across him. Her hair, a curtain of silk against his throat.

Branches broke in the distance.

Cal stilled, his muscles tight, unyielding. A moment later, two masculine voices barked over the din of the rain.

Julia froze. "Delgado's men?"

"I'm going to find out." He moved off her. "Stay here," he ordered in a toneless whisper. Quickly he slipped his shoes on, then slid his knife into his belt. "I'll be back in a few minutes."

"And if you're not?"

"I will be, I promise."

"What are you going to do?"

With her hair disheveled, her eyes wide with fear, he realized what he'd done. Who he was. What he'd told himself he'd never do. He was a killer.

And he never mixed his personal life with business.

This time, the pain made it easy for him to lie. "I'm going to lead them away."

"Liar," she whispered when he'd left.

Julia reached for her heart, rubbed the ache from beneath it, and realized she'd been wrong.

It had belonged to Cal all along.

Chapter Thirteen

Cal stopped short and raised a finger to his lips. Julia followed him quietly between the trees.

They'd gotten up early, both opting for little or no conversation. The previous evening still fresh in her mind. Cal gave her a quick sign for silence and to follow.

The dense brush opened into a clearing. At the far end stood a small man-made hut built up on a high foundation of beams.

In the middle of the clearing, under a grass-covered lean-to, sat a large wooden barrel.

Two men stepped from the opposite end of the clearing. Both carried a bushel of leaves. "Your friends?" she whispered in Cal's ear.

"Yes. His name is Miguel," Cal whispered. "His son, Robard, is next to him."

"Then why are we standing over here?"

"I want to show you something," he replied patiently, but his gaze scanned the perimeter. "And the best advantage to watch is from here. Miguel tends to be a little shy when it comes to strangers."

The men dropped their bushels onto the ground near the waist-high barrel.

"What are they doing?"

"Making cocaine," Cal responded in a low murmur.

"Those are the coca leaves. They're getting ready to mix the coca with ammonia and lime."

Julia watched them dump the bushel of leaves into the barrel of dark liquid.

"The barrel is filled with diesel gasoline," Cal commented. "*Used* diesel gasoline."

They watched the men stir the mixture. Each taking turns until the leaves were saturated. Julia noticed for the first time that the barrel sat on a long, narrow, wooden trench that ran about six feet in length.

After a while, the older of the two men unplugged a hole in the barrel and the gasoline streamed into the trench.

"The narcotic substance from the coca is in the gasoline. They're separating it for processing."

At the end of the trench was another, smaller steel tub that caught the coca saturated gasoline.

The younger man grabbed a gallon jug and poured it into the gasoline mixture.

"That's more ammonia. Watch. The mixture will turn to a white, milk-like liquid."

Julia watched as the white, cloudy mixture developed. Then while the young man stirred, the older one poured in more gasoline. "The gas forces the narcotic part of the plant to clump." A few minutes later both men scooped bowls full of the liquid into another barrel with a fine mesh material covering it to strain the white clumps of cocaine.

When they were finished, Julia was surprised to see only a few handfuls of cocaine drying on the cloth. "That's very little product for how much work they put into it."

"They earn very little from that. Most of the money goes back into the process. The cartel sells the gasoline, ammonia and other supplies at steep prices."

"Yet they still do this?"

"None of them wants to, Julia. They would rather grow

bananas, corn and other foods, but the market isn't good. So most produce gets thrown away unsold. They're forced to raise coca plants to survive. On regular crops they would barely clear a hundred U.S. dollars a month. Selling cocaine, they clear three times that much. The alternative is starvation."

The two men laid the cocaine out flat in the sun to dry completely. Soon they were starting the process over.

"The government cannot do anything. They send planes to make chemical drops to kill the coca plants, but the drops can only be controlled so much. The chemicals kill their other crops as well. The government has also promised to supplement the legal crops but there isn't enough money to go around.

"The cartel controls the government."

Laughter sounded, high-pitched giggles drifting from the grass hut.

Julia stiffened. "Do I hear children?"

Cal swore.

Suddenly, a barrage of bullets hit the air. Cal shoved Julia to the ground and placed a finger over his mouth telling her to be quiet.

Two gunmen stood at the rim of the clearing, AK-47s pointed at the farmers' chests.

"Stand away." The gunman's high-pitched voice and his companion's mottled complexion told Julia that both men were high.

A string of Spanish flowed between the men. "They want the cocaine," Cal interpreted quietly. "It seems they ran out and decided to bypass the middle man."

The two gunmen approached the farmers and forced them back against the gasoline barrel.

"Cal, the children." Julia couldn't keep the fear from her voice.

"I know." Cal took out his gun and waited. The gunmen directed the farmers to give them the cocaine drying in the sun.

"Stay here," Cal ordered softly. He maneuvered around to the hut and slid under its floorboard and porch. The position gave him a direct line to the gunmen.

Suddenly, there was a muffled whimper from above him. Through the cracks of the boards, he could see a boy and a girl, neither older than six, huddled in the corner. He placed his fingers to his lips. "Shh."

Suddenly, Julia appeared at the back door. She talked to them softly in Spanish, calming them, holding them.

So she understood Spanish. Anger whipped through Cal. He pushed back, knowing now wasn't the time. But later...

One of the gunmen prodded the men with the machine gun toward the dried cocaine. He demanded they put it into a bag.

Neither gunman gave Cal a clean shot. He whistled low, catching Julia's attention.

"Scream," he ordered in a low murmur.

Julia nodded and gathered the two children close. Quickly, she explained what she was about to do.

She took a deep breath and let out a bloodcurdling scream.

Startled, the two men stepped toward the hut. Cal's first shot hit the closest gunman in the forehead; he dropped to the ground dead. The other stopped cold, then swung his machine gun toward Cal.

Cal put three bullets in his chest. The gunman dropped his weapon and slowly sank to his knees. While Cal watched, he tumbled over. Dead.

"Papa!" The boy broke free first and shot out the hut's doorway. The girl instinctively stayed with Julia. She hugged her tight until the tremors of fear left both of them.

The little boy's father hugged him close.

"Damn it, Miguel. Have you lost your mind?" Cal asked in Spanish.

"West?" Miguel sat back against the porch railing and gathered his son to his chest. His eyes searched for his daughter, saw that she was safe in Julia's arms, then turned back to Cal. "What the hell are you doing here? Not that I'm ungrateful, *amigo.* Your timing is heaven sent."

"Coming to see you."

"You have excellent timing then, my friend," Miguel joked. He waved a finger toward the two dead men. "They have robbed us before. They killed my son, Philippe."

"When?"

"A few months ago. Maybe more. Time, it does not matter when you miss someone like I miss my Philippe."

"You should keep a rifle handy, Miguel."

"I cannot afford bullets with so many mouths to feed at home," Miguel argued. "Besides, they would shoot me as soon as they see a weapon."

Julia walked up with the little girl, who immediately slid onto Miguel's lap. "Are you okay, Papa?"

"Yes, *bella.* Are you?"

She nodded, then buried her face in her father's shoulder.

"We have not been introduced, *señorita,*" Miguel said quietly. His hand stroked the girl's hair.

"This is Julia Cutting, Miguel. I'm helping her find her husband, Jason. Delgado might have him."

"A pleasure, *señorita.*" Miguel patted the little girl's head. "This is my daughter, Lynette." Cal lifted the boy into his arms.

"And this is José," Cal added, and ruffled the young boy's hair.

Miguel nodded toward the younger man who approached the porch. "This is my other son, Robard."

"Pleased to meet you, Ms. Cutting." Robard smiled. He shook Cal's hand. "And really great to see you again, Cal."

"You too, pal."

"I am in both of your debt," Miguel stated, his tone serious. "Thank you."

"No thanks needed." Cal dismissed the comment and sat José back on his feet.

"We could not stand by and do nothing," Julia added.

"Yes, you could have. So many others around here do," Miguel explained. "If you help, more than likely you become the next target of Delgado's anger."

After setting his daughter on her feet, Miguel stood and slapped Cal on the back. "You are spending the night, Cal?"

"Are you offering?"

"If I did not, do you think Consuelo would let me back into the house?" Miguel laughed. A full belly laugh that nearly set the front porch rumbling. "Eat with us. There is a hut down the road from us that has been empty for a while. You can stay there."

"How is Consuelo?"

"Fat." Miguel laughed at the shock on Julia's face. "She is going to have my baby in another month or so."

"Bloody hell, Miguel. That makes six." Cal grunted.

"Five," Miguel corrected quietly.

"Six," Cal said firmly. "Philippe is still your son."

Miguel looked past his friend's shoulder. "You are right, *amigo*."

"You realize you do not have to populate the earth single-handedly," Cal observed.

"And why shouldn't I?" Miguel laughed again, shaking his somber mood. He looked at the setting sun. "Dinner is waiting for us."

"We need to get rid of your visitors, Miguel," Cal said and

nodded toward the two dead men. "We can take them to the river."

"You are right." The farmer glanced down at the children. "Go with Ms. Cutting back into the hut and wait for us. Once we are done it will be time to go home and introduce her to your mama."

"I'd like that. But please call me Julia," she corrected gently. Lynette slipped her hand in Julia's and tugged her along. A lump lodged in Julia's throat.

"I—I'll show you the way, Ms. Cut...I mean Julia," Robard said, his face flushed, his voice soft.

Miguel cuffed his son lightly across the top of his head. "Mind your manners, boy. Ms. Cutting to you. Keep your moon eyes to yourself."

"Yes, Papa." But Robard's eyes didn't leave Julia's face. Instead, he shot her a smile. One that showed the charm of the man soon to be.

"My son is infatuated," Miguel mused.

"He's fifteen. He doesn't know any better," Cal replied.

Miguel watched Cal's eyes stay on Julia as she walked back into the hut with his children. "You're forty. What's your excuse, *amigo?*"

Chapter Fourteen

Cristo Delgado forced himself to finish the last lap in his pool. Every day he made time for one hundred laps without fail.

He did everything without failing. He started by making his first billion dollars by the time he was thirty.

But now, at almost sixty, Cristo wasn't interested in money. While it was a great motivator for most, to him money was a tool. It allowed him access to the most beautiful women, the upper levels of the world's social circles and the ability to make influential men obey his orders.

Caesar, Genghis Khan, Alexander the Great. They destroyed civilizations to achieve greatness.

Cristo considered himself their equal. Extortion, murder, money—all brought power. And power made empires.

Of course, there are some who are incorruptible. Not many. The President of the United States being one.

But those who were not, eventually died.

His fingers touched the tiled wall. He tilted his head up out of the water and blew the air out of his lungs.

"We need to talk, Mr. Delgado."

He expected to see Solaris only, so it was a surprise when Renalto stood at the edge of the pool holding an oversize white towel.

"It's daylight. Aren't you afraid you'll be seen?" He hauled himself out of the water. In Cristo's experience, men like Renalto preferred dark corners.

"It's a chance I needed to take." Renalto glanced over, noting that Cristo's son sat at a table nearby. An electronic game in his hands and speaker buds in his ears. "Is he safe?"

"My son does not care about you, Renalto," Cristo retorted. "He is waiting for the car to take him to the mission. You can speak freely in front of him. He's involved in his games."

"I had the situation under control. There was no need to kill Leopold."

"Leopold was added insurance," Cristo replied. "I need you to make sure the DEA and Coast Guard do not interfere with my shipment. If you were suspected of treason, it would cause problems. Killing your friend and attacking your residence guarantees that Calvin West thinks you have not been compromised."

"The plan was for me to turn them in," Renalto argued.

"And that did not happen." Cristo shrugged. "Plans change."

"How in hell did I know he was going to take off in my car at the airport?"

Solaris stepped forward, a drink in one hand, sunglasses on his face, masking his eyes. He handed the drink to Cristo. "The guards have asked permission to clean Marsh up. Otherwise, the stench is going to attract unwanted attention."

"From who?" The orders were to leave him be and Cristo didn't like his orders, no matter how unusual, questioned. But he was a reasonable man. To a certain point.

"Delivery people, mostly."

"You take care of it," Cristo ordered, then took a sip of his gin and tonic. "Personally. Hose him down or something. I do not want anyone else near him. He is too...persuasive. I do not need him turning my guards against me."

"You might want to reconsider your order in the near future. West escaped to the jungle," Renalto cut in with impatience. "It won't be long before he tries to snatch Marsh."

"My point exactly," Delgado said tersely. "This should have been handled first at the airport, then today at the airstrip." He set his drink down and took another towel from a nearby lounge chair.

"Solaris blew the pick up at the airstrip. Jorgie at the airport."

"So my next question is why aren't you out looking for him?" Delgado asked and rubbed the towel over his wet hair.

"It's smarter to wait," Renalto insisted. "Searching for them in the jungle would risk killing them with a stray bullet. We need them alive until we find the prototype."

"Indeed. Correct me if I'm wrong, but wasn't it you who recommended paying off Alvarez's pilot so that we could take care of all this at the airstrip?"

"A miscalculation." Renalto shoved his fingers through his hair. "The pilot screwed up. He tipped off West somehow."

"And now?"

"Esteban killed the pilot then returned to his villa. Without the Cutting woman," Solaris stated. "She is with West in the jungle."

"We will have West and the woman. Do not worry, Mr. Delgado," Renalto assured him. "Within the next twenty-four hours."

"Worry? I am not worried, Renalto," Cristo said silkily. "You see, I understand what will happen to you if this minor hitch is not taken care of in a timely matter."

"I understand. West suspects Jason Marsh is being held here at the compound," Renalto advised him. "He will show up. We'll be waiting."

"Not you," Cristo corrected. "I have something more interesting for you to do."

"I like interesting," Renalto replied slowly.

Cristo's eyes flickered to Solaris, who pulled a cell phone out of his pocket. "I need you to contact my associate in Washington, D.C. He'll call you on that phone."

Solaris handed the cell to Renalto. "Don't lose it."

"I won't," Renalto assured him.

"We are running out of time. The shipment can only be delayed for a few more days," Solaris put in. "Any more than forty-eight hours will raise suspicions with the port authorities."

"I'll take care of the timetable," Renalto snapped back. "Once we get West and Julia Cutting we'll have the MONGREL."

"Any unusual delays and the port authorities will make sure it gets back to the Americans," Solaris indicated. "Captain Stravos won't be happy hitting open sea with that type of risk hanging over his ship."

"Check in with your people, Renalto. See if West has made contact with Cain MacAlister, then report back to Solaris." The fact that Cristo deliberately put Renalto at a distance using a middle man didn't escape Renalto's notice. "I'll be looking for West and the woman within the next twenty-four hours," Cristo said with a dismissive wave of his hand.

"Yes, sir," Renalto responded, then turned to leave, only to stop short on Cristo's next words.

"However, if he doesn't show, Renalto. I'll be looking for you. Understood?"

"Understood."

Solaris waited until Renalto left, then turned to his boss. "Captain Stravos could create a problem with our new timetable," Solaris commented.

"Damian can be controlled. Right now he is otherwise occupied. I've told Rosario to entertain the captain for the next few days."

Solaris flexed his jaw, but the giant's next words remained even, almost casual. "Is that wise?"

"It is necessary. Our deadline is moving closer." Cristo put on his sunglasses and lay back on the lounger, his face turned toward the sun.

Another vanity, Solaris thought with disgust.

A limo pulled up to the side of the house and honked. Argus stood and gathered his backpack. He walked over to his father and gave him a hug. "Goodbye, Papa."

Cristo tapped the boy's cheek. "Study hard. Impress the Padre Dominic and he will tell me. Then you will be rewarded."

"Yes, sir," Argus answered, the skin on his cheeks pale.

Solaris watched the ten-year-old walk away for a moment, smiling when the boy stomped his foot in a puddle by the pool.

It also reminded him of another issue to address.

"We may have a problem," the big man advised Cristo quietly. "I found footprints outside Jason Marsh's cell. It seems someone is visiting our prisoner."

"Did you take a look at the security log?"

"Nothing unusual showed up. But I made note of the shoe marks. I can trace them." Solaris stepped toward the puddle. He noticed the shoe print still wet on the cement. Small feet, narrow at the heel.

Brows drawn together, his gaze followed the boy until he disappeared inside the limo.

"Did you talk with Jorgie?"

"Yes. He assured me that none of his men would dare to break his orders to leave the prisoner alone."

"The cameras?"

"Nothing. Whoever it is knows how to avoid being seen." With a small swipe of his foot, Solaris rubbed out the print, then glanced once again at the retreating limo.

"Argus is returning tonight?" Solaris asked.

"Yes. I want him here. Then tomorrow he will stay with Padre Dominic while Rosario and I bring the captain from Caracas." Cristo paused. "Why?"

Solaris shrugged. "No reason."

"And this intruder?" Cristo demanded.

Solaris looked once again at the cement. "I'll be waiting for him tonight."

THEY'D WALKED FOR TWENTY MINUTES before they reached Miguel's home. Past dead crops of banana trees, fruit bushes that were no more than branches, and shriveled vines.

"Acid drops," Miguel said when he noticed Julia's glance. "A government program to kill coca plants. But they are not discretionary on which crops they kill. Many times they kill the wrong plants," Miguel pointed out. "So even if we could make money selling produce, the government has made it harder for us."

The house lay on the outskirts of a village of no more than a dozen houses. In a glance, Julia realized Miguel's home was twice the size of the other grass huts. Sturdier, its sides reinforced with discarded, broken lumber, its roof shingled with wood. But still much more primitive than Julia had ever seen.

A woman came out on the porch. Petite in stature, no more than five feet, with a big round belly and long, wavy black hair. A small baby girl, no more than a year old, sat on one hip.

"Consuelo, look who is here," Miguel boasted.

"Calvin West," Consuelo exclaimed, a big smile spread across her face only to turn into a scowl a moment later. "You did not come just for a visit. You came to ask my Miguel a favor, didn't you?"

Cal nodded. "Delgado has a friend of mine, *señora,* in his prison. Miguel has agreed to help me."

"Consuelo. I help my friend because he has helped us," Miguel scolded. "It just so happens that if Cal had not come today, we would be telling a different story. Robard and I were jumped by two of Delgado's men."

"What? And you did not tell me right away?" She shook a spoon at him even as her eyes skimmed over both her husband and children. "Anyone hurt?"

"No, Mama," the kids chorused.

Consuelo studied them for another minute, checking for herself. "Inside then and get washed for dinner." She handed the baby to Robard and waited for all four to go into the house. Then Consuelo spat on the porch. "That is what I think of Delgado."

"Do his men attack the villagers often, Miguel?" Julia asked.

"Often enough. Men and women are killed every week," Consuelo answered for her husband, the anger barely controlled. "My eldest son was coming back from the mission. He wasn't even helping Miguel that day. Still, Philippe got caught in the crossfire of Cristo Delgado's men and their target practice."

"Which men?" Cal asked.

"Jorgie and some others. They left my son's body by the river for the animals. They did not even bring him home."

Julia saw Cal's jaw tighten.

"Enough, Consuelo. You will spoil our guests' appetites," Miguel said, his tone soft, his words firm. "We will leave the past for discussion after our meal, *bella.*"

"Ha! Don't sweet-talk me, Miguel. I am not beautiful, with my belly it makes me the size of a cow." Still, she smiled.

"What is for dinner?" Cal asked, charming. The genuine

kind that she saw when they had first gone out together. Sadness squeezed at her chest.

The table was made of scratched, sturdy bamboo. The kids played with pots and pans in the corner.

The scent of flour, onion and chilies hung pleasantly in the air. "We have beans and tortillas with some chicken I bartered for with one of our neighbors."

She turned to Julia and Cal. "After dinner, I would like to find out more about your friend that Delgado holds."

Consuelo slammed the platter on the counter. "He is the devil. He owns more than the land. He owns the government. Controls most of the shipping. What he doesn't control, his friend Esteban Alvarez does." She held up a bowl. "We feed our children corn flour and beans because he takes the food to feed his belly."

"They do not own the church."

"Even Delgado would not take on that sin." Consuelo slammed the bowl down next to the plate.

"What do you mean?" Julia asked.

"Our old priest, Padre Dominic, runs the mission not too far from here. Shrine of the Little Flower. He and the other priests have taught our children for many years. Crime has escalated to such a point that we fear for our children, except at the school. The mission is the one place that does not get touched."

"Delgado protects the school? Is the priest one of Delgado's supporters?"

"Padre Dominic?" Consuelo snorted. "No, but he does try to keep the peace."

"He is my uncle," Miguel added. "My mother's younger brother. He protects the children. And their parents."

"Cristo Delgado is afraid if he does not respect the church, bad things will happen to his empire."

"He sends his son there to show the people he is one of us," Miguel explained. "He believes we are that ignorant."

"But he is kept isolated from the rest of the children, Miguel," Consuelo corrected. "He is given private lessons from the priests."

"Delgado pays for the boy to be taught. Padre Dominic uses the money to pay for the other children's supplies."

"The boy is not one of us, Miguel. Robard says Argus Delgado stays to himself. He makes no friends at the mission with the other children. He will be like his father."

Julia hoped not. "How far is the mission from Delgado's villa?"

"Not far. A mile or more through the jungle. Five miles by road, if they aren't washed out."

"Everyone sit now," Consuelo said and placed a bowl of chopped bananas and oranges into a bowl.

"My wife, she works at the villa. In the laundry three times a week," he explained to Julia and settled the baby into her high chair.

"Have you heard about a new prisoner, Consuelo?" Cal asked. "A man by the name of Jason Marsh?"

Consuelo shook her head after a moment and handed him a plate of beans and gestured to the table. After Cal placed it in the center, he took a seat next to Julia.

Consuelo settled next to the baby and waited for the other children to sit. Then she started filling their plates. "The laundry is filled with gossip every morning. The guards flirt with the younger girls and sometimes mention the business of the villa. We older women listen very closely." She stopped for a moment and caught her Lila's hand before she put bananas into her hair. "But I have heard nothing of your friend."

"Then he is dead, I'm sure," Miguel said without preamble. He grabbed a tortilla and took a bite. "No one talks of the dead."

AFTER DINNER, THE MEN TOOK THEIR conversation outside. Robard led the children into the back room for bed.

Julia wandered to the door, hoping to catch a word or two. Cursing herself for giving up her secret fluency in Spanish. Had she not, they'd be talking in front of her.

"It is no use trying to eavesdrop. They do not want us to hear what they are planning," Consuelo commented, disgusted. "We bear children, teach them, love them, then watch them die. Yet, dealing with the devil is too much for us to handle," she scoffed.

The baby fussed. Without thinking, Julia picked her up and cuddled her against her chest. She remembered how Cal treated the younger children at the cocaine site, and later played with them after dinner.

This wasn't a man who could harm a boy like Argus.

"Cal wants into Delgado's compound," she said absently and hugged the baby.

"Unless he is a woman, he is not allowed past the grounds. Only women work inside the villa."

"Why is that?"

Consuelo smiled. "Because they believe we cannot do them harm."

"I know a couple of women who would do them serious damage." She thought of her friend, Lara Mercer, the President's daughter, who also had been one of Labyrinth's operatives.

She placed her cheek against the baby's head, felt the soft tuft of hair tickle her cheek.

"How did you and Miguel meet Cal?"

"A similar situation like you saw today," Consuelo answered. "Philippe and Miguel were buying supplies from Cristo Delgado's men. The gasoline and ammonia mostly. Jorgie showed up with his men and started threatening the men with guns. Cal showed up out of nowhere and started shooting up their cars from the bushes. Had Jorgie chasing his tail trying to find him in the jungle."

Consuelo laughed and shook her head. "Jorgie lost a lot of power that day. Cal showed many of us Jorgie's stupidity."

"Emasculated him, but didn't kill him," Julia reasoned. Much more damaging to Cristo's chain of command.

"Jorgie would have been better off if Cal had killed him, I think."

Julia agreed. Something she was sure Cal was aware of when he let Jorgie live. "Consuelo, do you think you could get me inside?"

"It is dangerous. There are cameras and guards positioned all over the compound." The other woman stopped for a moment and thought. She glanced at the men outside. "What you are doing, will it save the rest of my children from being harmed by Delgado and his men?"

"Yes," Julia replied with conviction. "If we succeed, it should put Delgado and anyone like him out of business for good."

"And to do this, you need to find Jason Marsh?"

"Yes," Julia said. "If he is there somewhere in the villa, we need to get him out."

"All right. We can do that," Consuelo agreed after a moment. "But we must act quickly. Tomorrow morning."

"You have a way in?"

"Yes. But it is risky," Consuelo considered. "But less risky for us than the men. They will have to stay behind."

"That's it then." Julia glanced out of the window. "I can't see Cal agreeing to any kind of plan that doesn't include him."

"Then we won't ask him," Consuelo answered, her eyes on the chopping knife. "If I am injured, I will need assistance. We will dress you in my clothes and darken your skin with henna. With your eyes and hair, you will pass."

"And the men?"

"By the time they realize we are gone, we will be back. And with your friend, Jason."

"I'm almost afraid to ask," Julia admitted. "But how are we going to manage sneaking away?"

"Easy." Consuelo reached for a jar in the cupboard. "Leave it to me," she smiled, holding up the brown spotted leaves. "And don't drink the coffee."

Chapter Fifteen

Rosario entered the veranda of the villa. The apathy brought on by the wine was wearing off. The starkness of the sunlight faded, diffused by the evening chill. But the rays still cut into her, making her eyes smart, her skin prick.

"Join me for a walk?" Solaris stood to the side, in the shadows, enjoying her scent of jasmine and soap.

Rosario started, then instantly relaxed. "Why not?"

"I talked with Cristo today."

"He told you about Stravos." It was a statement, not a question. "Did Cristo tell you I said no?"

"But you changed your mind."

"Cristo changed it for me," she admitted bitterly. "With veiled threats and—"

"Did he hurt you?"

"No." Comfortable that the bruises were well hidden beneath clothes and makeup, she did not hesitate to lie.

"Let Cristo think I will do more," Rosario stated, disgusted. "Captain Stravos is a squat little man with bad manners and very little intelligence. I can handle him."

"He is a man with some power and many connections. That is enough," Solaris commented. "I will help you. Protect you. Just say the word."

"You are asking too much. Cristo would see you killed, Solaris. And I don't think I could bear that."

"Yet you bear his beatings, his insults." Solaris's anger deepened his voice. "You are his wife, but he treats you worse than his whores."

"But he does not force himself on me," she said softly, her hand on his arm soothing. The strength of it beneath her finger-tips comforting. "Also, I have my son to think about."

Temper warred with common sense. She wanted to rage at Delgado. Tell him his precious son belonged to another man. But in her position, she understood the fine line she walked. What it would cost Argus if Cristo ever discovered the truth.

"He has a daughter also. Will she suffer the same fate as you?"

"Argus seems to think so," she commented.

Cristo never mentioned Alejandra. When the girl returned, she could only imagine what her father had in store for her. After all, if he can pimp out his wife…

"Do not fool yourself, Rosario. Cristo expects you to welcome the advances of Captain Stravos," Solaris continued.

"I will be charming and keep the little man happy. I will ply him with wine and a good cigar. Find him a nice place to pass out when he's had too much. I will not let him touch me."

"That is good. Because if he did, I would have to kill him," Solaris promised.

"Cristo killed his first wife, didn't he?" Rosario asked quietly, finally putting her worst fear into words.

"Yes, he did."

"And he will kill me eventually, too," Rosario considered. But anger infused her next words. "He thinks."

"No," Solaris vowed. "That he will not do. Not while I am here."

"And you will stay here," she replied, her confidence

born from the love between them. "With me, until my son is grown."

"Your son has been keeping company with our prisoner, Jason Marsh," the giant commented. "You wouldn't know the reason for that, would you?"

"Why should I? Cristo took him down to see the man shortly after he captured him," Rosario replied after a moment. "Argus told me he liked Jason. They share common interests."

Solaris swore. "And you didn't object, Rosario?"

"What should I do, follow my son down to the tunnels? Tell his father?" she snapped back. "In many ways, he is like his father, Solaris. I can only tell him not to do something. That is all. Whether he listens to me, is up to him."

"He shouldn't be down in the cellar. He might get hurt, or worse."

"Yes, I know." Rosario frowned. "Jorgie might discover him there and he will tell my husband."

"Cristo knows of the visits, but not who was visiting. I didn't know it was Argus until after I reported the incident to Cristo."

"And now?"

"Keep him away from Marsh, Rosario. Or he will suffer the consequences," Solaris warned. Then he stepped in front of her, blocking her from anyone who watched. Slowly, he raised her right sleeve, exposing her wrist. Dark purple bruises mottled the delicate skin. The giant's eyes flashed with anger but he did little more than let his thumb skim over a few of the marks. "And no one knows better than you, the damage Cristo can do to his son when displeased."

"Argus understands, too, Solaris," she murmured and looked at the walls and the gates surrounding their home. "Thank you for the walk."

The giant bowed, dropped her wrist and walked away.

THE MORNING SUN SLICED ACROSS the top of the security wall. Jorgie pushed his sunglasses higher. Pain shot through his forehead. He scowled and pinched his nose between his thumb and forefinger. The damn thing hurt like a son-of-a-bitch.

He dropped his hand to his side, promising himself that if he ever got his fists on Calvin West, the man would suffer more than a broken nose.

A feral smile twisted his mouth into a cruel jagged line. If there was something that Jorgie specialized in, it was dishing out pain.

It was one of many jobs he performed for Cristo Delgado, along with being in charge of the villa's security and the drug lord's personal bodyguard when necessary.

But the two responsibilities he considered perks were torturing prisoners for information and keeping an eye on the locals.

Which included inspecting the servant shifts everyday.

Many of the local women spent their lives working hard, yet never rose above the country's poverty. Many sought a way out, even if that way meant sleeping with Delgado's men.

As head of security, Jorgie never lacked for female company.

He made it a point over the last few years to recognize everyone who worked for the villa and their families. It was he who Delgado turned to when disciplinary actions were required. And he knew that his boss was always impressed when Jorgie could recall the names and faces of those Delgado chose to punish.

Jorgie watched Consuelo approach through the gates. Pregnancy only enhanced the exotic features, her round belly swayed with feminine stride, igniting a fire that burned deep in Jorgie's loins.

Once Jorgie had acted on his desire for the woman. After

her shift, he'd ordered his men to bring Consuelo to his bed. But before Jorgie could get his hands on her, Solaris countered his order and told Consuelo to go home to her family.

Then in no uncertain terms and in front of his men, the giant told Jorgie that he was not to touch Consuelo. Miguel's association with Padre Dominic would make it difficult for Delgado if the priest found out about any abuse.

Solaris had warned Jorgie that if anything happened to the couple, Solaris would hold him personally responsible.

Jorgie hated being ordered by anyone but Delgado himself, but he didn't dare go against the mercenary. Instead, he chose a different way of showing his displeasure. He used Consuelo's oldest son for target practice. And took great pleasure in the fact that Solaris could do nothing when he'd found out. Jorgie claimed the boy walked in the path of the bullets.

A lie of course. Jorgie and his men jumped the boy, shot him and left the body where the family would find him.

And laughed all the way to the cantina.

Jorgie straightened from the wall. He noticed a new girl followed Consuelo through the gate. The wind plastered the white cotton sleeveless blouse and dress against her. He caught the graceful sway, the long legs silhouetted beneath.

Jorgie smiled. Things were looking up. He stepped in front of them both.

"Who is your friend, Consuelo?"

"This is my cousin, Maria," Consuelo answered stiffly. She held up her hand. Gauze covered her from wrist to her finger-tips. "I hurt myself this morning. Maria is visiting and offered to help me do laundry tonight, so I would not be replaced. We need the money, Señor Jorgie."

Jorgie took his knife from his belt and slit open the gauze. Underneath the bandage was a wound at least three inches in length. "How did this happen?"

"Cooking. My baby distracted me with her cries and my knife slipped. If I get it wet, I will need stitches."

Jorgie understood that most of the locals did not see doctors. It was far too expensive.

"Uncover your head girl and look into the light," Jorgie ordered Maria.

The woman removed a wide red scarf from her head and looked straight at his chin. Her hair was tied back in a short, silken ponytail, leaving her features unobstructed.

Beautiful.

"Report to my office after your shift with your cousin, Maria. I will need to ask you more questions. Understand me?" Jorgie looked at Consuelo, daring her to object.

Maria put her hand on Consuelo's arm, stopping the pregnant woman from saying anything.

"Yes, *señor,*" Maria answered, her voice a mere whisper.

And subservient. Jorgie felt the heat rise from between his legs and looked forward to spending time with the woman alone.

"As soon as my shift is finished."

"Not a minute later," he warned.

Chapter Sixteen

Lavender silk and brocade draped the windows of the bedroom, pooled at the bottom on moss-green carpet. Tapestries of all sizes and bold hues covered the pillows and shaped overstuffed chairs.

Argus loved his mother's room. One of the few rooms in the mansion that held warm memories. He'd played on the floor, rolled in the sunshine that spilled across the rugs.

"Mama?" He walked quietly to the oversize bed, not wanting to create any unwanted sound. His mother was extremely sensitive to loud noises.

He touched her shoulder, grateful for the warmth beneath his fingertips. His greatest fear would be to find her cold. And dead.

A soft groan reached him. Brown eyes blinked, then steadied on him. But drugs had left them bloodshot and foggy, the rims of her eyes puffy and smeared with mascara. His father's drugs.

"Are you all right, Mama?"

"Yes, my darling." The words were slurred. She struggled to sit, but the covers weighed her down. "What time is it?"

"The evening. You missed dinner so I was concerned." He leaned over and kissed her cheek, blocking out the sour scent of sweat and wine.

"What day is it?"

He adjusted her pillow behind her head. When he was done, she took his hand and pressed it against her cheek.

"Wednesday," Argus replied. "Father said you and he will be going into the city tomorrow to fetch Captain Stravos."

"That is true." Reluctantly, she let go of her son's hand and patted the space on the bed beside her. "Sit next to me for a moment, Argus."

"I only have a few minutes, Mama," he warned her gently. "Papa will be upset if I am late for my studies."

"Your papa is busy, he will not know," she scoffed. "Just be the clever boy I know you are and don't get caught, Argus."

"I won't," he promised. "Will you be okay while I'm gone?"

"Yes, *mijo*. I will. We are returning soon after. This will not be a long visit." She kissed the back of his hand. "And you?"

"Papa's driver is taking me to the mission tomorrow. I will be staying with Padre Dominic for a few days. I promised to help him with the new shipment of supplies for the locals."

"That is probably for the best. I worry about you getting into mischief down in those tunnels."

"I like him, Mama."

"I know you do. But Solaris is aware that Jason Marsh has a visitor. You must be careful there, too."

"I will be."

"I know you will, *mijo*." She closed her eyes and dropped her hand from his. Within moments she was asleep again.

Argus felt the fear trickle through him. He tucked the blanket around her and left the room quietly. Afraid or not, he needed to take care of her and his sister.

"REPORT TO ME," JULIA MIMICKED with derision. "Over my dead body."

"It just might be if we are not careful," Consuelo insisted.

"You must watch for the cameras and avoid them at all costs. We will have to leave with the first group and hope he does not see us from his office."

"And where is it?"

"The first floor, near the security barracks." Julia pulled out a crude map of the compound and villa that Consuelo had drawn for her.

"Would he be holding Jason there?"

Consuelo shook her head. "No. They usually hold enemies down in an old cellar they converted into prison cells. But it is hard to get to, and heavily guarded when he has a prisoner there. But no guards have been down there for about two weeks. Not one."

"Two weeks," Julia repeated, considering. "Exactly two weeks?"

"I believe so, but I would have to check with others to make sure. Why?"

"Maybe Delgado is keeping them away from Jason on purpose."

"If that's so, he must not believe that your friend is in any condition to escape."

"That's what I'm afraid of."

THE TWO MEN HIKED THE DISTANCE from the grass hut to Delgado's compound in record time. Sometimes running through the jungle when they hit a clear path, but mostly hacking through the dense brush and overgrowth with machetes.

Just as the sun sank beneath the treetops, Cal found a position that overlooked the front of the compound.

Miguel held the binoculars to his eyes. "They should be coming out soon. An hour at the most."

Cal nodded, preferring to monitor the compound through the sight on his rifle. "If they don't, we're going in."

Miguel slowly lowered the glasses and studied his friend.

"I haven't known you for a long time, Cal. But I know about men and women. The anger is coming from more than frustration. It's coming from the heart, is it not? Or worse, maybe. Like mine, it is coming from fear."

"It's coming from the fact that Julia has no regard for her own life, damn it," Cal snapped. "And the fact that I'm supposed to keep her safe in spite of herself."

"Do not get me wrong, Cal. I'm not happy with Consuelo, either. But both women are intelligent. They might be taking a risk to free her husband—"

"Ex-husband, damn it."

"Ex-husband," Miguel corrected, then glanced at the ground, hiding the tug of a smile. "But they are doing no less than what we were planning on ourselves. And using a more clever cover. After all, Consuelo does work for Delgado. Maybe we should be patient and wait to see how successful they are before we go charging in like two fearful lovers."

THE SCENT OF DECAYED EARTH AND human waste thickened the air into a fetid tar that choked Julia's lungs and clung to her skin.

She clawed at the walls, cringing when the slime slicked her grip, the brick cut into her fingers.

Consuelo had warned her to expect the worst. That the whispers of the servants were filled with fear and tales of rotted bodies washed with blood.

The cellar had two entrances. Each led to a maze of underground hallways.

The first entrance was located deep within the villa's kitchens at the back of the main house. The other entrance was outside. Not more than twenty feet into the compound's courtyard at the base of the villa's southern wall.

Julia decided instantly that it would be easier to enter

through the kitchen, simply because the household servants didn't carry machine guns. The courtyard guards did.

Actually, she navigated the mansion with little problem. She made no eye contact, made no conversation. She kept her head down, her hands filled with a basket of linens, her feet moving at a swift pace. If the security cameras picked her up, she would look like most of the women that worked at the villa.

It had taken Julia most of the day to sneak away from the laundry room. Consuelo reminded her to be back before the compound's siren marked the end of the shift in an hour. Otherwise, she'd be caught for sure.

An hour wasn't much time.

The kitchen proved a little more difficult. Not wanting to draw attention, she put the basket under a nearby serving table, then managed to stay within the corners and crevices of the room and hallway until she reached the entrance.

Julia reached the bottom of what must have been two dozen steps and studied the narrow, bricked tunnel.

At the end, a light glowed a dim, jaundiced yellow from an old bulb that hung from the ceiling on a single, thick wire.

Quickly, she made her way to the end, her nerves jumping in tempo with every step. Whispers bounced off the walls. Julia froze, her ears strained. A small rush of air tickled the back of her neck.

The hushed tones were urgent, almost fearful. Slowly, she crept forward. The passage split into a fork. The words were almost distinguishable, but the echoes did little to tell Julia their origin.

Julia continued, choosing the passage on the right. It took little more than ten feet before she realized the voices were fading, lost through the walls of the tunnel.

Dread filled her gut but she reversed her steps and followed the faint sound.

JASON MARSH SHIFTED ON THE CEMENT. The cold crept into his muscles, made them stiff. His shoulder throbbed. Delgado's men had dislocated it, leaving it useless.

How many days had it been now? Seventeen? Had it been a week since the last beating? Jorgie did such a good job, Jason fell unconscious halfway through. He had no idea how many hours he'd lost before he woke again.

Almost three weeks either way. They hadn't found the MONGREL. Otherwise, he would be dead by now.

In the still of the cellar, he heard the soft whisper of rubber against dirt.

"Jason?"

"Argus," Jason whispered, his lips crusted with blood, cracked open and bled. "I told you not to come down here anymore."

He struggled to his feet, sucking in air as bone ground against bone. He gritted his teeth against the pain, then pulled his chains until he reached the prisoner bars. "If your father catches you down here—"

"He and Mother are leaving for Caracas tomorrow morning. Right now, he can't be disturbed. He is busy with last minute details," the boy said, obviously parroting his father's words. "And Mother is…sleeping."

Sleeping? More likely passed out somewhere, Jason thought.

The boy was tall, thin and gangly, with pointed shoulders and a long, thin nose. His hair stood like a bristle, neatly trimmed to an inch of his scalp. Designer labels marked his clothes. The blue jeans alone probably cost more than most farmers made in the area in a year.

Jason caught the picture of Bach on the front of the boy's T-shirt. Argus loved classical music. He enjoyed playing the piano whenever he could. Usually when his father wasn't around.

Cristo saw music as feminine, a threat to Argus's masculinity and in essence a threat to his empire. An empire he was grooming his son to rule.

Over Jason's dead body.

Argus Delgado shoved a woven bag through the bars. "Eat this. Quickly. I need to bring the bag back with me. It's cheese and bread and bottled water."

"You'll have to hand it to me, pal. I can't maneuver the whole bag." Jason lifted his injured shoulder slightly.

"That reminds me," Argus said. He reached in his jeans pocket and pulled out a bottle. "Aspirin from my mother's bedroom. For the pain."

"Thanks." Argus opened the bottle and shook a few of the capsules into Jason's palm. Jason swallowed them dry. "Start with the water."

Argus handed Jason the bottle. Slowly, the agent drank, ignoring the pain that rifled through his sore jaw and throat. "You still need to go, Argus. I don't want you discovered with me."

"I had to come and warn you, Jason," Argus insisted in hushed tones. "Father told Jorgie you would be dealt with when he gets back. He also told him that I'm to watch and learn how to handle someone who interferes with our family business. It is my reward for doing well with my studies."

A ten-year-old being trained to torture. The nausea roiled through Jason, this time from more than a bruised stomach. "What is he planning?"

"He is flying to Caracas to take care of a shipment of cocaine, but he has also gone to get your wife. She is here in Venezuela."

Jason froze. "Give me the details, Argus. Everything you know."

"That's just it, I know nothing else." Argus paused. "I didn't know you had a wife, Jason."

"She's my ex-wife."

The boy nodded, and took the bottle back. He slid the food through the bars. "She has something called MONGREL," Argus remarked. "Papa calls it the Drug Hound."

"That's what it is, essentially." Jason leaned against the bars, but left the bag dangling between his fingers. How in the hell did Delgado find out about Julia?

"What is the MONGREL, Jason?"

"It's a device that's no bigger than a cell phone. It can detect your father's drug shipments through the steel hull of any ship," Jason explained. "A sort of ultrasound that can break down compounds to microscopic sizes."

"He said you stole it from your own country," Argus continued. "Why?"

"I had my reasons, pal," Jason explained. "But I'm not planning on letting your father have it."

The boy frowned. "No wonder my father is angry."

"What else did you hear, Argus?"

"My father met with a man this morning. Someone I have never seen before." Argus frowned, thinking. "They mentioned Julia was here with a man called West. And we're making plans to set a trap for both of them here at the villa."

"West? Calvin West?"

"I believe so," Argus stated, his voice picking up with excitement. "Is he a friend of yours?"

"No," Jason said, his mind already working through the details. "If Julia somehow makes contact with you, Argus, I need you to do whatever she says. Understand me? There's a good possibility things are going to get really ugly around here, and she'll keep you safe."

"And Calvin West?"

"Don't trust him. Only Julia."

"Can Julia help us protect Alejandra? She'll be graduating soon from college. Father will insist she return here."

"I'll help your sister, pal. But first I need to stop your father's next shipment. Then stop your father."

"The shipment's been delayed. Father instructed my mother to keep Captain Stravos entertained," Argus said, his voice tight. "He hit her until she agreed...."

Argus couldn't finish.

Jason understood. "I know it seems a little hopeless right now, Argus. But we'll save your mom and your sister. And if we're lucky, save ourselves in the process."

"And your wife, too?"

"Ex-wife," he corrected without thought. "Yes, her, too."

"What do you need me to do?"

"It's time to get the keys for my chains and the cell door. Do you think you can?"

Argus frowned, concentrating. "Father keeps his set locked up in his office. With him gone, it should be fairly simple."

"Just be careful. Don't risk getting caught. I'll find another way out."

"I'm to spend the next few days at the mission with Padre Dominic, but I can manage to return earlier," Argus explained.

"How?"

Argus shrugged. "There is a way but you'll have to wait until tomorrow morning."

Jason studied the boy and couldn't help the pride that shifted through him. "Tomorrow it is then."

"Even if I help you escape your cell, the guards have been doubled on the grounds. It will be very hard for you to sneak past them injured."

"Leave that to me, pal." He shoved the food back through the bars toward Argus. "Time for you to go."

"Okay." But when the boy started to leave, Jason stopped him.

"Argus, did you happen to catch the name of the man who met with your father this morning?"

"Yes. His name was Renalto."

Chapter Seventeen

Julia followed the voices, but lost them in the maze of hallways. She'd heard enough to know that one was a man's, the other a boy's.

Jason? Her heart thumped hard against her chest, making it difficult to catch her breath.

She stumbled down the nearest passage, praying she wouldn't run into a guard.

Suddenly, the stone steps appeared at the end of the narrow corridor. Below lay another passageway.

Pushing away her fear, Julia took a step through the small entrance underneath the stairs.

The ceiling hung low, forcing her to duck her head. After a few feet, a doorway gave way to a wide open room with several prison cells lined across one side.

Chains rattled softly, permeating the fetid air.

Quietly, she made her way toward the sound and stench.

In the corner of the farthest cell, she saw him. Her breath caught at the back of her throat.

He sat in the corner with no shirt. His head rested back against the wall, his eyes closed in the semidarkness. Only a pair of tattered slacks covered his legs and no shoes.

Her chest constricted. She was too late; he was already dead. "Jason?" Her voice barely carried across the cell.

Suddenly, a stream of expletives hit the air. On their heel, chains rattled. Jason struggled to his feet.

"Oh, my God," she whispered.

His face was mangled almost beyond recognition. Both eyes were nearly swollen shut, his shoulder misshapen. Black bruises peppered his chest, arms and stomach. A large sickle-shaped cut slashed his cheek from his left eye, down to his jaw.

Julia remembered the knife Jorgie was cleaning his nails with, sure the wound was his handiwork.

"What the hell are you doing here, Julia?"

"What?" The anger hit her like a tidal wave. So much for grateful. "The hell if I know," she snapped out. "I thought I'd bring my camera, maybe catch a few moments of you being tortured and then head on my happy way."

"You know what I mean," Jason argued. "You promised to get Argus out of here. Not me. You should be at the mission."

"I found you first." She looked at the lock on the cell door. You would think you'd be grateful—"

"There is no way in hell you can get me out of here. Trust me, if it was possible I would be long gone. You're jeopardizing the plans. What if Cristo finds you? Or worse, Jorgie?" Jason asked. He looked past her shoulder toward the tunnel. "Where is West?"

"Not here," she bit out. "Consuelo and I drugged her husband, Miguel, and Calvin. We left them sleeping back at Miguel's."

"You what?" Jason swore. "Look, the directions were simple. Get Cal to bring you here. Make sure he leaves you at the mission when he comes to rescue me. If you drugged him, he's not going to trust you. You need that trust. Or he won't leave you at the mission by yourself."

"Damn it, Jason. I'm trying to do what I promised. But it's not as simple as you are making it out to be—"

"What do you mean—" Jason stopped and stared at Julia. "Have you slept with him?"

"That's none of your business," she snapped.

"The hell it's not!" Jason answered. "I don't need West getting territorial over you right now."

"You don't need…" Julia stepped up to the cell. "You are just as bad as he is. Giving out orders, using me to get what you want."

"There's a difference, Julia. I'm using you to save my son," Jason replied quietly. His tone reminded her of the man she used to know before this. Before their marriage.

Her heart softened. "Then trust me to do it, Jason."

"I'm trying," he muttered.

"Try a little harder," she argued. "I'm going to tell Calvin about Argus. And where I hid the MONGREL."

"No." Jason gripped the bars with his good hand and leaned in until their faces were mere inches apart. "You will not tell him about my son. Or the device. Understood?"

"Calvin isn't going to harm Argus, Jason. If you can't trust him, trust me."

"Cal will hand Argus over to that bastard Cain to use as a weapon against me or Delgado."

Julia shook her head. "You're wrong."

"No, I'm not," Jason insisted. "Padre Dominic will get you safely out of the country with Argus. Calvin isn't part of the equation. The only reason we used him to get you here, was the fact that Padre Dominic couldn't take the risk of picking you up at the airport and bringing you here himself."

"I know. And he was right," Julia answered. Quickly, she told Jason about her arrival and Cal's confrontation with Jorgie, Cal's meeting with Esteban and the airport gun battle.

"And you still think Cal will protect Argus?"

"Calvin thinks that a mole in Washington gave Cristo your plans."

"Did you say Renalto met you at the airport?" Jason's head snapped up. Julia heard his grunt of pain.

"Yes," Julia affirmed. "Why?"

"Does Renalto know you're headed to the mission?"

"I don't think so. Originally he was supposed to help Cal breach the villa and rescue you. But after we escaped the attack at the airstrip, Cal decided to bring me here."

Jason swore.

"Jason," Julia said urgently. "What's going on?"

"Renalto's dirty. He's working with Delgado. He's being paid to help capture you and West." Jason paused. "If I'm right, Renalto informed Cristo you were coming with the MONGREL."

Jason gripped the bar. "Do they know that you have the device?"

"No," Julia answered slowly, considering her next statement. "But I don't exactly have it anymore, either."

"What do you mean, you don't have it?"

"I won't let it end up in the hands of the bad guys, Jason," Julia explained. "So I left it with a friend."

Jason placed his forehead against the bar, disgusted. "That was my collateral, Julia. My get-out-of-jail-free card."

"Cal will get you out of here," Julia argued. "I know he will. That's why Cain sent him here, and that's what he's determined to do."

"You're wrong. Cain didn't send Calvin here to save me." Jason laughed, his tone brittle and dry. "He sent Calvin here to kill me. Because that's what Calvin West does. And he's the best in the world at what he does."

"I don't believe you." Julia bit back the scream of denial, but something deep inside stopped her. Cal, an assassin?

"His code name says it all, Julia." But this time she saw the pity in her ex-husband's eyes. "It's Thanatos. The Greek God of Death."

SIRENS PIERCED THE AIR, ECHOING through the dark halls beneath the villa.

"Get out of here, Julia. Take a left out from beneath the stairs, the first right and another left. You'll find the stairs to the courtyard," Jason ordered. "Get my son and get the hell out of Colombia. I'll take care of Calvin."

"You're wrong." She took one last look at him, turned on her heel and raced out of the room.

A few moments later, she sighed with relief when she found the stairs. Quickly, she raced to the courtyard, then deliberately slowed her pace when she hit the outside air.

The sirens ceased, but the vibrations remained, setting the birds in flight and the air humming with electricity.

The tip of the sun crested the treetops but the sky grew more gray, then black. Big drops of rain spat at the ground, beat a rhythm of warning on the tree leaves—with each minute Mother Nature picked up the storm's tempo.

Still, the compound grew active. Women lined up at the gate, getting checked before they were allowed to leave.

Julia spotted Consuelo toward the rear of the line, lagging behind; her eyes darted over the courtyard until they rested on Julia.

Julia lifted her hand to wave but her friend's gaze slid past Julia's shoulder. Consuelo's features twisted in fear.

CAL SCANNED THE CROWD THROUGH his rifle scope. "Bloody hell."

"They're not in line?" Miguel focused his own binoculars. "The guards check off everyone. If they aren't there, Jorgie and his men will go looking for them. We can't let that happen, my friend."

"It won't. Even if I have to go in and drag her out by her hair," Cal vowed. But the fear slithered through his gut, snaked up his spine.

A woman appeared from the far side of the villa, her steps graceful but swift as she hurried across the courtyard. Her head covered with a shawl, protecting her from the rain.

"It's Julia," Miguel announced, the relief evident in his voice. "She's headed for Consuelo and the gate."

Suddenly, Jorgie strolled out his office and snapped an order to one of the guards. Within moments, another guard grabbed Julia's arm and held her.

"Damn it." Cal didn't hesitate. He dropped the binoculars and grabbed Miguel's machine gun. "Once Jorgie has her in the building, we won't be able to get her out."

"What are you going to do?"

"Cause a diversion," Cal said. "You get as close as you can to the gate and be ready. When the women start running, you snag ours, then head back to your house."

"And you?"

"I'll follow soon enough," Cal promised, his voice hard. "Just make sure you all get back safe."

"Aren't you going in the wrong direction, *señorita?*" Jorgie jabbed a finger toward the barracks. "I asked you to report to me after your shift."

"Please," Julia reasoned, and pushed the fear back deep into her stomach. The guard tightened his grip, prodding her to answer Jorgie. "My family will worry if I do not come back with my cousin."

Jorgie laughed and stepped closer. His finger trailed slowly down her jawline.

Without warning, he backhanded her. Pain exploded through her jaw. Razor-sharp stars jabbed behind her eyes. The guard tightened his grip to keep Julia on her feet. She wiped her hand across her mouth, tasted the metallic bite of blood against her tongue.

"You seem to think I am asking your permission, *se-*

ñorita," Jorgie said, his tone harsh. "I am not. You will only be here a few hours and if you please me, I will pay you overtime." He pinched her chin, raised her face up to his until they looked eye to eye. "Give them the money or keep it, I don't care. Understand?"

"I can't—"

Gunfire exploded behind them. The guard let Julia go with such force, she stumbled to the ground.

Jorgie yelled orders and his men dropped to their knees, raised their machine guns and opened fire on the surrounding jungle.

Women screamed and scattered.

Julia staggered to her feet, her face throbbed. Ignoring the pain, she ran toward Consuelo, who held the gate open.

"The hills!" her friend screamed. "We must run into the trees!"

THE SHADOWS GREW UNTIL THEY swallowed what little daylight remained.

"Come on, Julia. Hurry." Consuelo grabbed her under the elbow and helped her through the dense foliage. Suddenly, Miguel appeared.

Relief swept through Julia, making her weak. Consuelo embraced her husband. Gave him a quick kiss, then whispered in his ear. Miguel looked at Julia's face. He swore.

But Julia had no concern for bruises or Miguel's reaction. Instead, she scanned the trees. "Where's Calvin?"

As if to answer, a burst of gunfire exploded behind them. Far enough away for Julia to understand Cal was still near the villa.

"He's keeping Delgado's men pinned so we can get away," Miguel explained. "Let's not waste his efforts."

Julia tried to struggle but realized her strength had left her. "We must help him, Miguel. Please."

"He doesn't need our help. He needs not to worry about you being in harm's way. If he is distracted by you, he'll get himself killed."

"But—"

"He's already seen you beaten, Julia. It put him in a rage. He must believe I will do as he asked and get you to safety with my wife. He will meet with us back at my home. I promise."

Julia tried to nod, but the darkness overpowered her. The last thing she heard was more gunfire.

CAL COULDN'T PUT THE IMAGE OF JORGIE striking Julia out of his mind.

Damn it, he cursed himself. She was breathing, running. The hit in the face wasn't lethal. Still, the frustration, the fear slithered through him, threatening to break his concentration. Cal inhaled slow and deep, working through the emotion, concentrating on the sounds of the jungle.

The first time he killed had been in this same area. The sounds of monkey chatter, the buzz of the insects.

His target had been a young kid barely out of adolescence, only a few years younger than himself at the time. With acne, no less. But still old enough to run illegal arms. Old enough to sell explosives to third-world countries at war. Explosives used to kill women and children.

An easy kill at one thousand yards. One shot to the forehead. Two to the chest.

After a year or so, he lost count.

A metallic click of an assault rifle ricocheted off the trees. Heavy steps pounded through the thick of the vines and branches. Cal crouched in the shadows and waited.

Soon, one of Delgado's soldiers stepped past.

Cal slid his forearm around the man's neck, shoved his head far to the right. He heard the snap, felt the body go lax.

Waited. A short breath desperately taken through a broken windpipe.

Cal settled the dead man in the undergrowth. Quickly he retrieved the boot dagger, ammo and equipment vest. He grunted when he discovered infrared goggles attached to a strap, a flash bomb clipped to the dead man's belt.

Cal put as much distance from Julia as he could manage. He secured the infrared goggles and the flash bomb, knowing Solaris and his men would also have them. Good, he thought.

He'd been in this situation before. On the run in city streets, in the mountains.

But the scent of the rooted vines and dirt brought back intense memories of his run from Solaris years earlier. And the first time Cal had met Jason Marsh.

Solaris had him dead on the river's edge.

Then without warning, gunfire broke from the jungle. Most of Solaris's men collapsed, riddled with bullets. The others dove for cover.

Solaris took a hit in the stomach. The force knocked him back into the river.

Cal managed to crawl to a break in the brush for cover before the blackest part of his pain carried him over the edge into unconsciousness.

Soon after, he awoke in the cave. It was there he met Jason Marsh for the first time.

In blackface and camouflage gear, the deep-set eyes held an edge of insanity at first glance. But within a few minutes, Cal realized it was an edge of anger, the heat of revenge that inflamed those eyes.

"What the hell were you thinking, West?"

Cal stiffened. "Do I know you?"

"No, but you're MI6 and way out of your league here, mate." The man dropped to the floor and checked Cal's wounds. "Jason Marsh, DEA."

Cal looked past the camouflage paint. "You're one of Solaris's men."

"Not anymore. I just shot the son of a bitch. I consider that a resignation, wouldn't you?"

Jason reached into a nearby first-aid kit.

Cal raised an eyebrow.

"Took it off a dead compatriot," Jason said. He pulled Cal's thigh bandage free. "I removed the bullets from your leg and side, but you're going to have to find a doctor. One that isn't in Delgado's pocket." He opened a small bottle of alcohol. "This is going to hurt like hell, but it's all I have to stop the infection. No noise."

Jason poured the alcohol over the open thigh wound. Fire exploded, shooting Cal to the pits of hell and back. He struggled through the worst of it with gritted teeth.

"This cave is far enough away from the river, you won't be discovered. Give you a few days to recover."

"What are you doing here?"

"Deep undercover. And I was right there, too, under Delgado's nose. You owe me for this, West."

"Maybe I can help you get back in."

"I haven't shown up. They'll think I'm dead."

"Or wounded," Cal reasoned. "I'll shoot you."

"No thanks—"

"If I put a bullet in your leg or some other non-vital organ, you'll stand a better chance. Give it a day or so, then show up wounded. Hurting and maybe a little delirious."

"Might work," Jason acknowledged his lips grim, his brows drawn. He handed Cal his pistol, grip first. "Remember, nothing vital."

The crack of gunfire brought Cal back to the present with a start. Swearing, he slid through the muck, using a handful to blacken his face. Ignoring the taste of foul vegetation in his mouth.

Jorgie broke through the brush. His arrogance or anger driving him to charge through trees shouting orders to his men.

Cal shoved the infrared gear to his forehead and reached into his bag for the flash bang stun grenade.

He blinked, allowing his eyes time to adjust to the darkness, his ears tuned to the sound of men crashing through the jungle.

When Jorgie and his men burst into the clearing, Cal threw the stun grenade. The explosion split the air. On its heels came the loud, painful cries of the men in range, now blinded by their infrared gear.

Cal grunted. Jorgie lay in the middle of the men, unconscious. He thought to finish it, but he understood others were nearby. Silently, Cal withdrew, understanding it would've been better if Jorgie had died and saved Cal the trouble of killing him later.

It took Cal several hours to reach Miguel's home. Not near the time he needed to cool his anger and fear from the last few hours.

Several times he stopped and backtracked to make sure he hadn't been followed.

He opened the door without knocking.

First thing he saw was Julia sitting at the table, dressed in a clean navy blue muscle top with the word Corona across the chest and a pair of loose black cargo pants that hung low on her waist.

"I'm fine," she said, but her hand rested nervously against her face, not wanting him to see the damage.

Consuelo stepped forward. "Cal, I took care of it. It looked worse than it really was. The swelling will go down quickly."

Cal's gaze didn't leave Julia. He removed her hand from

her cheek and let out a long hiss between his back teeth. "I'll kill him."

She saw it then, underneath the rage. The fear. "This wasn't your fault, Cal—"

"You're bloody hell right it wasn't. It was yours," he snapped. "And you can bet we're going to discuss what 'stay put' means when you and I are alone."

She straightened her spine, indignant. "Care to hear what I found out?"

"No, I don't," Cal said. "Right now, we need to deal with the fact that Jorgie is less than two hours behind me." Cal turned to Miguel. "He'll suspect Consuelo's involvement with this. He'll come here first to ask questions. He'll be looking for Julia."

Consuelo visibly paled. "Why would he question me? I was injured and brought my cousin here to help. That is all. It is not unusual to bring in relatives to help."

"Your timing is too coincidental. When was the last time anyone attacked the compound?"

"No one has," Miguel answered, his features grim.

"Because it's suicide. Jorgie will realize the gunshots were a diversion. It won't take him long to figure out the rest and end up here."

Cal glanced at Miguel. "You must leave. You and your family need to get out of the country."

Miguel shook his head. "We have no place to go."

"We can go to the mission," Consuelo suggested. "Padre Dominic will help us."

"No, our family is too large for my uncle to hide," Miguel stated in a hard tone. "Jorgie will search the mission. And if he finds us, he will take us to Delgado and most likely kill my uncle in the process. An attack on the villa might be enough for Delgado to ignore his superstitions and attack the church."

"I agree with Miguel. You can't risk being found," Cal told them.

Consuelo nodded, but was visibly shaken. Her face pale, her hands trembling. Julia placed a comforting arm around her shoulder. "Don't worry, we'll think of something, Consuelo."

"I already have," Cal answered. "But I need something to write with."

Consuelo found him a pencil from the other room. "Memorize this, then get rid of it." Quickly, he wrote a phone number down on a card, handed it to the other man. "Can you get your family into Caracas by tomorrow, Miguel?"

"Yes," Miguel said. "I believe I can."

"Good," Cal replied. "Once you're there, call the number. Call collect. The man who answers is a friend of mine. His name is Renalto."

"Not Renalto, Cal," Julia interrupted. "Jason told me today that Renalto met with Cristo. That he's not to be trusted."

"And if I tell you Renalto can be trusted, no matter what Jason thinks," Cal replied. "Who will you believe? Me or your ex-husband?"

"Is this some sort of test?" Julia snapped. "You are risking Miguel and his family."

"I guess I have my answer," Cal replied. He turned to Miguel. "Tell Renalto you are in trouble, that you helped me and now you and your family need covert transportation into the United States. We have a contact in Washington, D.C., by the name of Cain MacAlister. He and Renalto will take it from there. You understand?"

"*Sí,* I understand, *amigo.*"

"Don't ask for help from anyone else," Cal warned. "Too many people are Delgado's paid informants."

"I won't," Miguel agreed. "And what will you and Julia do? You cannot stay here, either."

"The mission," Consuelo suggested. "Padre Dominic can hide them easily enough, Miguel."

"It will be too dangerous—"

"My wife is right, Cal," Miguel interrupted. "Julia is in no shape to escape through the jungle. My uncle will have no problem hiding you."

Cal glanced at Julia, saw the fatigue in her features.

"Go to the mission," Miguel urged, then he reached out and shook Cal's hand. "When you find my uncle, tell him I am in need of a vacation. He will understand."

Consuelo stepped up to Cal and placed a soft kiss on his cheek. "Thank you."

"*Amigo,* if there is any way I can return your favor, please let me know," Miguel said sincerely.

"There is one thing," Cal replied. "When you contact Renalto, tell him to meet me northwest of the villa in twenty-four hours. Tell him to bring his arsenal with him."

Chapter Eighteen

Padre Dominic Seymour was no longer a young man of twenty. Balding and dressed in a long cassock, he was more than three times that age and it showed.

Thunder cracked and lightning flashed through the mission window, destroying the shadows of the old building.

The mission had been built from rocks and cement. Its tower, absent a bell, still loomed over the adobe roof. Cracks and faded white paint webbed the walls, showing the mission's age, its losing battle against the elements.

The bell at the front door clanged, but not unexpectedly. He had already heard of the attack on Delgado's villa earlier. Understood many of the locals were afraid. And when they are afraid, they seek reassurance from the mission.

Still, Padre Dominic had learned in those forty years to be cautious, especially when greeting those at the door. Most came for charity, others for blessings, but some to steal what little the mission held.

He swung the large door open. "Hello?"

"Padre Dominic?"

"Yes?" A man and woman stood at the step, their clothes wet, rivets of water ran down their faces.

But even in the lantern glow, the woman was beautiful.

The man's features were more defined, the eyes dark, cynically so.

"I am a friend of Miguel's. He sent me here, hoping you could help us."

"Miguel?" Padre Dominic did not move from the doorway, but he gripped the pistol a little harder. "And how is my nephew?"

"He told me to tell you he is in need of a vacation."

A smile broke over the older man's features. "I am glad."

He pulled his hand from his pocket and revealed a small pearl-handled pistol. Quickly, he set the safety and returned it to his pocket.

When Calvin glanced down, Padre Dominic smiled. "Sometimes a bit more than prayer is needed on a dark night."

"I understand," the man responded, his mouth lifting into a small, polite smile. One that did not reach his eyes.

"Please come in out of the rain." Padre Dominic stepped back into a large entryway of stone and tile.

"Excuse the lack of light," he said, slightly raising the lantern. "Our generator decided to die tonight of all nights."

The woman rubbed her arms against the chill.

"May I ask your names?"

"Calvin West," the man said without preamble, then he nodded to the woman. "Julia Cutting. Miguel told us that you would give us shelter for the night and Julia shelter for the next few days while I take care of some business."

"We would be willing to pay, Father," Julia said.

"Well, I never turn down a donation, but it is not necessary." He turned toward a large room on the right. "Come this way. I have a fire going and some blankets in our community room. You'll be more comfortable there."

The room itself was large. At least twenty feet long and just as wide. Two love seats sat in front of a huge stone fireplace. Flanked on either side were nearly a dozen straight-back chairs.

Several paintings of men, presumably saints, decorated the walls. Above the fireplace hung a large wooden cross.

Once they were settled onto a love seat, covered by the blankets and close to the fire, Padre Dominic went to the wall and pulled on a rope. "Excuse me if I seem inhospitable, but I would like to know why you seek shelter here."

"I have a friend who might be held prisoner in Cristo Delgado's villa. I came here to find out and to rescue him if possible."

Another priest appeared, his demeanor quiet, slight in stature with sharp features. "Yes, Padre Dominic?"

"Padre Mateo, could you please make up two of our guest rooms in the south wing?" He glanced at the couple. "Also make sure some hot tea and the leftover stew and bread from our evening meal is brought to their rooms."

"It will be my pleasure." The priest turned to leave when Padre Dominic stopped him. "Please take care of this your-self. Do not tell the others that we have guests. No use rousing them from their sleep. I'd prefer to keep it to ourselves for now."

Padre Mateo bowed his head. "As you wish, Padre."

After the younger priest left, Padre Dominic turned to Calvin. "He is a good man."

When Calvin raised an eyebrow, Padre Dominic decided to ease the younger man's suspicions. "His family was killed by Delgado's men, Mr. West, when his father refused to cultivate his crops for cocaine. Rest assured he will keep your secret."

"Thank you for helping us, Father," Julia said and pulled the blankets tighter. The warmth of the fire took the chill from the room. "Miguel mentioned that this isn't the first time you've protected someone from Delgado's men."

"Unfortunately, more than there should be," Padre Dominic

admitted. "But sometimes we are too late. All I can do is pray for some and bury others."

Anger filled the older lines on the priest's face. "We have a cemetery that's located halfway between here and the villa. Its ground is full of men, women and children who could not escape the wrath of Delgado and his men."

"Maybe soon his own body will be buried there," Cal suggested.

"With God's blessing, of course." Cal studied the older man before him. Saw the experience that hardened his features, shaped the determination in the dark eyes.

"I have heard about your friend," Padre Dominic stated. "Some who come to Sunday services whisper about the villa's comings and goings." He rubbed his nose. "It will not be easy to save him, Mr. West."

"I know. That is why I would like Ms. Cutting to stay here with you, under your protection. Miguel assured me that Delgado and his men leave your mission alone."

"We must let you know, Father, that Delgado is looking for me," Julia said. "He thinks I have something he wants. Something that can stop his drug operations. My presence could be putting you all in jeopardy."

"There are worse things I am afraid of, my child. And none of them scoundrels like Cristo Delgado." Padre Dominic smiled. "But you are right. His man Jorgie visited us earlier. He and his men searched the grounds and the rooms. Of course they found nothing."

"They could come back. Once they find Miguel's house deserted."

"Are he and his family unharmed?" the padre asked.

"They are heading on that vacation we spoke of. They're going to visit some very trustworthy friends of mine in Washington, D.C."

"That is good," Padre Dominic said, pleased. "Of course

you could be right about Jorgie coming back. But I think the chances are very unlikely. The fact that Cristo let him search here once is a surprise. Cristo has a terrible fear of the church. One that his mother instilled in him as a young child. She was what you would call a fanatic. Preached brimstone and fire. But it is a fear that I do not mind taking advantage of on occasion."

"I hope you are right, Padre," Julia commented.

"Come, I will show you to your rooms. Rest easy tonight. No one will seek you in this weather." Padre Dominic rose slowly.

"After morning prayers," Padre said, his eyes on Julia, "we can discuss your plans for the immediate future."

ONE CANDLE LIT THE ROOM, GIVING it just enough light to reveal the long shadows, the severe angles of the concrete wall, the spiderweb cracks on the dull brown linoleum floor.

The red and blue and yellow patchwork of the bed quilt stood out, the only splash of color provided in the stark room.

A pine nightstand with a simple whitewash basin and pitcher of water and a couple of towels stood on the opposite side of the bed. And in the far corner stood a solitary chair with a pair of white cotton drawstring pants and a matching white T-shirt.

Padre Mateo had left a tray of soup and bread on the bed; its strong scent made Julia's stomach grumble.

The wind whistled, finding its way through the gaps and crevices of the wall. She slipped off her shirt and pants. A shiver danced across her skin, but not from the chill of the evening.

She'd planned on waiting until Calvin left before she talked again with Padre Dominic, but now she wasn't sure.

In less than twenty-four hours she would be on her way back to the States with Argus.

And a hundred things could go wrong before now and then. A hundred things could go unsaid.

The past few days had shown her what kind of woman she could be.

The kind who took risks. The kind who walked into a guarded compound without a weapon. The kind who chased the man she loved across a field riddled with gunfire.

And she did love him. And tonight she would take another risk.

He'd leave in the morning. But unlike the last time, his departure would be expected. No echoes of hurt or betrayal accompanying them.

Quickly, she washed up with the cold water. She slipped on the pants and shirt, shivering, but from nerves or the cold, she couldn't be sure.

Either way, her decision had been made.

Cal stood just outside the door. He'd made no sound but she sensed him nonetheless.

As if she'd willed it, the pine door swung open.

His gaze pierced the darkness, his body tensed. Without warning, he shut the door and then stepped toward her.

He wore identical loose cotton pants low on his hips and a plain white T-shirt that stretched tight across his chest.

His eyes cut through the semidarkness, lingered over her face. "Julia, nothing will have changed come morning." His hand slipped behind the base of her neck, rubbed the tender skin with his thumb.

I will, she admitted silently.

"I understand," she agreed in a low, husky tone. "But tonight…" With deliberate hands, she slipped out of her T-shirt and pants. "Nothing between us."

He growled deep in the back of his throat. Her arms snaked around his neck as she pressed her body to his.

Her hips shifted, cradling him intimately, until she felt him shudder against her.

His hand traveled down her spine, drew lazy circles with his fingertips. She arched farther into him.

He gripped her butt, brought her in tight. She gasped at the suddenness, the sensation of hard against soft.

Her eyelids fluttered, then closed, her head fell back against his shoulder. Unable to resist anymore, Cal touched his lips to hers, felt them tremble. His body screamed to take her with the insanity that plagued him but something in him resisted. Something in him needed to show her the gentleness, the—love.

Desire flooded him. He cupped the back of her neck, brought her close as his mouth delved deeper into the soft, warm recesses of her mouth. His tongue traced and caressed until she stretched up against him, her body pressed against him, begging him silently for more.

Julia felt his shirt scrape softly against her breasts, the rough cotton abrasive and erotic against her nipples.

She drew his T-shirt up and over his head, groaning when he was forced to break contact.

The scent of the rain, the moisture clung to them both. The bare skin of his chest and shoulders gleamed in the dark of the night. Slowly, almost cautiously she ran her fingertips over his collarbone, following the indents at the base of his neck. She felt him swallow against her touch and her mouth curved with pleasure. She'd forgotten how much he liked to be stroked.

Her fingers trailed down the bare skin of his chest, stopping every few seconds to trace the indentation of his ribs, the ridges of his torso.

"Enjoying yourself?" The words came out in a low rasp, but he didn't stop her progress.

"More like reacquainting myself," she answered, the teasing lost in her own breathlessness.

The other times he'd taken control, shown her, led her, taken her where he'd wanted to go. This time, if it was to be the last time, it would be the way she wanted it to be. Take him where she wanted him to go, be with him every step of the way.

She slipped her tongue between her teeth, licked his skin in short velvety strokes. He groaned even as he buried his hands in her hair, urging her with the slightest pressure to continue.

She pulled the knot loose on the drawstring of his pants. "Julia—"

"Shh," she whispered. She cupped his arousal, desire snapped at her nerve endings. He was hard and ready. The heat of his passion radiated from his body, but still he held himself tight.

Panting, her breath hot against his stomach, she slipped her hands around his hips and under his waistband and slowly followed the hard contours of his butt, his thighs, until both his pants and briefs lay in a pool at his feet.

He was rigid and hard against her cheek. The scent of his arousal flooded her senses. Her need to taste him almost painful but she held herself for a moment, suspended in time, enjoying once again the power she had over him.

He didn't beg, but Lord knew Cal wanted to. He didn't recognize this woman kneeling before him. Teasing, tormenting him.

In the darkness, he could see her tongue play against the edge of her teeth, as if she was anticipating the taste of him.

Cal growled.

Julia laughed wickedly, thickening his blood, setting his body throbbing.

Then her mouth was on him. Hot, tight, stroking.

Cal's knees nearly buckled under the pleasure.

Her fingers circled him, squeezing just enough to give more pleasure than pain. This time he fell to his knees.

"Enough," he rasped. His arms circled her and he snatched her against him, stopping her torment, but intensifying his.

He fell back onto the ground, taking her with him, cradling her against his chest.

She sighed and stilled, content to have the hard security of his arms around her, his body curled around her in protection. Suddenly, Cal shifted her up until her breasts were level with his mouth.

"My turn," he whispered, just before his mouth caught a nipple between his lips. This time Julia shuddered as pleasure raced through her. She moved restlessly against him as his mouth nibbled and stroked. His fingers found her secret spots between her thighs.

Without warning, his fingers slipped into the damp, dark heat of her. Stroking her from the inside, taking her to the edge with his mouth and fingers.

"Cal?" She fought against the urgency that seized her.

"Don't stop it. Let it go," he whispered, his breath hot against her ear. With his free hand, he cupped her chin, forced her to look at him.

His eyes were wicked black, his lids heavy with desire.

His fingers stoked her, his thumb finding the sweet spot between.

She whimpered, unable to stem the flood of heat that rushed and pooled between her thighs.

She tightened against his hand, gripped his shoulders and rode the tidal wave over the edge.

"I'll give you a few seconds, sweetheart."

But the orgasm only whetted her appetite for him, for the feel of him inside her.

Frustrated, she shifted until his hips bumped against hers.
"Now." His arousal probed the apex between her thighs.

Then he was in her, filling her, taking them both over
the edge.

Chapter Nineteen

Julia woke up in her bed alone; still, her hand searched the pillow next to her. No note. Nothing.

He'd left in the middle of the night. The same as last time.

Quickly, she dressed back into her now-dry clothes.

The storm had passed during the night, and the clean scent of the morning was left behind. She glanced out of her window and froze.

The first thing she saw was a young boy sitting at a bench, reading. His head down, his shoulders rounded.

Quickly, Julia opened the door and retraced her steps to the outside. It only took her a few more moments to find the boy.

"Excuse me," she said softly in Spanish. "Could you direct me to the Padre?"

"Sí, señorita." The boy was a handsome devil, with eyes the color of forest moss and a mop of hair that hung in an unruly sweep across his forehead and shagged around his ears. "But the priests have started morning prayers, so we cannot disturb them for another hour or so."

When he shoved the bangs back with his fingers, she smiled, instantly taking a liking to the boy.

Julia sat next to him. "What is your name?"

"I am Argus Delgado," he said with a small hesitation.

Hiding her surprise, she held out her hand. A moment later, he clasped it and shook.

"I'm Julia," she said, deliberately leaving out her last name. "It is a pleasure to meet you, Argus."

Startled, the boy continued to stare. "Thank you," he said, then glanced behind her. "Julia, may I ask where you have come from?"

"Originally, from Washington, D.C.," she said, testing the waters. Something tugged at her heart.

"Are you here on vacation?" Argus asked after a moment.

"Not really. I'm here to do a favor for a friend."

"I see," the boy said considering her answer for a moment. "Washington, D.C., is a very small distance from New York City, isn't it?"

"That's right."

"I have a sister in New York City. She is in college, studying law."

"That's a coincidence," she admitted. "I was a lawyer once, a long time ago."

"I know," the boy confessed.

Julia frowned. "Can I ask how you know?"

"Because I think your friend is also my friend. A man named Jason Marsh," the boy answered. "Am I right?"

"Yes, Jason is my friend."

"The favor involves me, doesn't it, Julia?"

"Yes, Argus, it does."

"If you are planning on taking me from my mother, I cannot allow it."

Julia saw the set of the boy's features, saw what she knew in her heart all along.

"Then I guess we go to the villa and get your mother, Argus."

The shock brought his eyebrows up under his shaggy bangs. "You will do that for me?"

"Yes, but you need to listen to me first, all right?"

"Sí," he said with excitement.

"I have another friend. His name is Calvin West. He's also a friend of your fath—" She stopped, realizing what she was about to say. "Of Jason's. I need him to help us. Is that all right?"

"You started to mention my father. Does he work for my father also?"

The boy was smart.

"No, he works for the U.S. government. He is one of the good guys," she reassured him.

"My father has many 'good guys' on his payroll, Julia. Some who work for the U.S. government and others who are even friends of Jason's."

"I know. But Cal isn't one of them. We need to find him, Argus."

"Where is he?"

"On his way to the villa, I'm sure." To possibly meet Renalto.

"I can get us there, but we have to go on foot," Argus said. "And we must leave before the priests are done with their prayers."

THE WIND TOSSED THE LEAVES AND vines—a flag of warning that a storm was building over the hills. Argus moved with amazing agility, but then of course, most kids knew their own backyards. Argus was no different.

"How much farther?" Julia stopped for a breath and put her hands on her hips.

"Only a few more yards. We have a cemetery with a small mausoleum. We can hide in there and rest if you need to."

"I thought I told you to stay put."

Julia jumped, her scream caught in her throat.

She turned around and saw Calvin dressed in different

clothes. Fatigues. A machine gun strapped to his back and a pistol in his hand.

"Where did you get all of that?" she asked.

"From someone who didn't need it anymore," he answered in a flat tone. "What the hell are you doing here?"

Julia put her arm around the boy. "This is Argus. He helped me find you. We need to make sure he and his mother escape Delgado tonight."

"I am Cristo Delgado's son." The boy said the words matter-of-factly.

Julia studied Cal, saw the truth hardened in his features. She realized she did trust him. Had all along.

"They're in danger, Cal," she said softly. "Help me save them."

"Let's go then," Cal said, his tone low. "We'll sort this out later."

The boy led them down a short set of stairs to a door. Slowly he lifted a dead bolt from across the way. Cal blinked, clearing the grit from his eyes. He studied the surrounding shadows. Stale fetid air filled his nostrils.

His gaze shifted over the room. It was small. No more than ten-by-ten. The wall was lined with tarnished plaques and cement squares. Cal stepped closer. Saw names and dates.

Tomas Sanchez. 1908 to 1940. Died with honor.

"It is a crypt, Señor West."

Cal smiled, his lips lifting with genuine humor. "I figured that out, Argus. Do you come here often?"

"Yes. No one else ever comes here. They are afraid it will bring bad luck to them and their family. I spend much of my time here."

In the corner were stacks of hard covers and comic books, candles and pillows.

Argus pulled out some matches from one of the books and lit two of the candles.

"You've got quite a setup here, pal."

Pleased, Argus's lips spread into a wide grin. The shadows deepened the features, making him appear older, similar...

The same set of the jaw, the same curve of the mouth, the broad forehead.

He glanced at Julia, saw the truth in the way her eyes skimmed the boy's features.

"Bloody hell."

CAL DELIBERATELY KEPT HIS expression emotionless, but the anger burned in his gut. "Argus, how did you and Jason become friends? Was it after your father arrested him?"

Argus shook his head. "No. One day he came to the mission. He worked with Padre Dominic to raise money for the people in the area. A secret he kept from my father. I, too, helped Padre Dominic. We kept the same secret and became friends."

"What did you do together?"

"We talked about different places, books. Many things."

"Did you talk about technology?"

"No," Argus replied, confused. "But we did discuss me visiting him in America."

"How long have you been friends, Argus?"

"For almost a year. Then he disappeared. He told me it would be a while before he could come back. The next time I saw him was right before Solaris arrested him. Maybe two days before. Jason had promised to take care of my sister. My father does not like her. I don't know why. But I'm afraid he might hurt her like..."

"Does he hurt your mother, Argus?"

"Yes."

"Did Jason give you anything? Like an MP3 player or a cell phone."

"Cal, he doesn't have it," Julia snapped, impatient.

"Why wouldn't he?" Cal asked. "Obviously, he and the boy share more than a special bond, don't they?"

"Yes," Julia answered solemnly. "Jason told me before he returned here. He made me promise not to tell you."

"No surprise there," Cal commented, but for the first time with no malice. "You've made no secret of where your loyalty lies, have you?"

"It lies with you," she argued. "I was going to tell you last night, but we—"

"I wouldn't mention last night," he bit out.

"And why not?" Then it dawned on her, the role reversal she found herself in. "This is how you treated me, Cal. When you stole my files. The situation is the same. But this time you're on the receiving end."

For the first time, she could see why he did what he did. Even if she didn't approve of his methods.

"No, Julia, it's not the same," Cal said, the anger brimming over. "I took those files to save your life, damn it. Just like I'm trying to do now. Delgado found out about my intentions to kidnap his son and he put a contract out on my family."

"That's why your parents suddenly retired? That's why you haven't heard from them? They're in hiding?"

"Yes, and why I need Delgado under lock and key."

Julia frowned. "But what does that have to do with me?"

"He also took a contract out on my lover. A contract he withdrew after he found out that same woman was no more than a pawn I used just to gain access to top secret government information."

"Oh, my God." Julia's knees buckled, forcing her to sit down on a nearby stone casket. "Why didn't you tell me?"

Slowly, disbelief turned to anger. "Why, Cal?"

"Jon and I decided there was no need to frighten you. I had already come up with the solution."

"You solved the problem." Her fists tightened, but the fury still showed in her face.

Argus took a step back. "Are you okay, Julia?"

"Fine, Argus," she reassured him, struggling to keep the rage from overpowering her voice.

She stepped toward Cal, deliberately crowding him. "So you and Jon Mercer made this big choice for me." She waved her hand in the air. "You just couldn't trust to tell me the truth. Or trust me to decide how *I* wanted to handle a threat on *my* life."

"It had nothing to do with you, Julia—"

"What?" This time her fists came up between them. "Of all the arrogant, stupid—"

"I saved your life, damn it!"

"You broke my heart, damn it!"

Silence hit the air, exploding around them. Tears pricked the edge of her eyes, but Julia refused to give in to them. "And when you did that, Cal, it hurt me far more than anything Delgado could've ever done to me."

"You have no idea what he's capable of." His jaw flexed.

"No, but now I really do know what you are capable of, don't I?"

"I chose to do the right thing, Julia. Whether you believe it or not."

"That's just it, Cal. You made the choice and left me none." Julia shook her head, suddenly tired. "Can I ask you something?"

"What?" But the word came out exasperated.

"Did you tell your mom about the contract on her life?"

Cal studied her for a moment. "Yes, I did. I told both my parents together."

"I just wanted the same consideration," she said sadly.

"Julia." Frustrated, Cal swore. "There is a big difference.

My father is retired military. He had a right to know in order to protect his wife."

"So it makes all the difference. Them being married," Julia concluded.

"It does," Cal replied. "They had each other to worry about."

"I guess my problem is that I thought we had each other, too."

Cal frowned, but didn't reply. There didn't seem to be anything left for him to say.

"Julia?" The voice was little more than a whisper. "If we are going to rescue my mother, we must hurry."

"I'm sorry, Argus." Julia placed her arm around the boy. "You're right, of course."

"You are not going to rescue anybody," Cal ordered.

"We have a solid plan, Cal."

"I can get us in, *señor*," Argus said. "I could have freed Jason a long time ago, but did not have a way of getting him out of the villa and away from here. My father has too many men. Too many people at the airports and in the city."

"So how has that changed?" Cal demanded.

"Julia said you are here to rescue Jason. While you are doing that, we can find my mother and leave. No one will be interested in us, they will be searching for you. If we are asked, my mother can tell them she is worried about a possible shooting and is taking me to the mission."

"And Julia?"

"We can hide her in the car very easily," Argus reassured him.

The boy was smart. Cal had to admit, it was a sound plan, but far more risky than if Julia and Argus left right away.

"I'm not going to risk your life or his, Julia," Cal said. "Argus, can you draw me a map of the villa? And show me where your mother's rooms are on it?"

"Yes, sir. But it would be much easier if I showed you."

"No, not this time, son. I need you to take Julia back to the mission. I'll bring both your mom and Jason there."

Julia stepped between the boy and Cal, then nodded toward the corner. "Is there paper and a pen you could use, Argus?"

"I don't know," the boy said slowly, then glanced from her to the books.

"Please try, while I talk to Calvin a moment." Julia pulled on Cal's hand for emphasis. "We'll be right outside."

"All right." Argus frowned, but stepped over to his corner.

When they reached the shadows just beyond the door, Julia pushed the door closed and turned to him. "Cal—"

"No." His eyes snapped to hers. "I will not risk a ten-year-old's life. I don't care if he's Jason's son or not."

"Jason told me differently. He said you wouldn't care about the boy. You would use him any way you needed to gain control of the MONGREL. He told me your code name was Thanatos. The God of Death."

Cal stilled. "Did you believe him?"

"I believe your code name was Thanatos. I never believed you would consider killing a ten-year-old boy."

"You told me once that you trusted me, Julia." Cal grabbed her shoulders and pulled her close. "Trust me now to handle this."

"I don't know, Cal—"

The door slammed shut, hit by the wind.

Startled, Julia frowned. "I thought we closed the door—"

Cal swore. "Argus."

They quickly searched the darkness, but already knew the young boy was gone.

"What was he thinking?" Julia worried.

"I'm sure he decided it was taking us too long to save his mother. And that he could do a better job," Cal said and returned to the muted light in the chamber. He pulled his gun out of its holster, checked the clip.

"We'd better follow him."

"We?"

Cal gave her a curt nod. "Just stay close, or I'll give you bloody hell when we're done with this."

DAMIEN STRAVOS HAD MORE THAN enough time to enjoy Rosario's charms.

She'd worn a white flowing sleeveless dress that skimmed her curves and showed off her ample bosom.

While he himself did not do cocaine, he made sure that it flowed free in the living room where they drank their wine.

"Where is your husband, Rosario?"

"He's been called away on business but should be back later tonight. I am truly sorry, Damien, that he is not here and that you are stuck with me." Her lips moved into a pout that set Damien's blood on fire.

"No, no. I understand that your husband is a very busy man. He must be gone a lot, with all his business dealings and such."

Rosario raised a delicate brow. Did this man really think she was that gullible? The pig.

He sat there with food on his shirt, and good wine in his belly. That's all he would get from her tonight.

Damien licked his lips. He'd had enough. Cristo had made it clear what kind of entertainment he was going to get tonight. Unfortunately, Rosario, while putting on a nice show, was not living up to Damien's expectations.

"Lock the door, Rosario, and then come sit," he suggested, then patted the couch cushion next to him.

Instead, Rosario walked over to the bar on the other side of the living room. "Would you like some more wine?" She held out the decanter.

"No, I'd like to stop playing games."

Rosario shrugged and filled her glass.

"What games, Damien?" She placed the decanter back in its place. "I thought we were having a nice conversation," she commented, her lips moving into her blandest smile before she took a long swallow of her wine.

Damien reached her in four quick strides. He grabbed her arm and drew her in for a kiss.

"Stop." She jerked her head away. Wine sloshed between the two of them.

Damien's grip tightened. "Enough! Lock the door and we'll finish what you've started."

Rosario struggled to get away. "I would like you to leave."

"Before the evening is through? I don't think so." The captain laughed harshly. "Your husband negotiated you as part of the shipment, Rosario. I intend to exact my payment tonight."

With his free hand, he gripped her hair and yanked her head back until her lips were only inches from his.

"I am not responsible for Cristo's deals or debts," Rosario bit out.

"But you are responsible for your son, are you not?"

Rosario stilled. "What do you mean?"

"Maybe you will reconsider your position tonight once I tell you that I know Argus is not Cristo's biological son."

"That's a lie," she said, but fear shook her voice.

"The doctor that delivered your son is a very good friend of mine. A friend that doesn't hold his liquor very well," Damien taunted. "He told me Argus needed a full transfusion at birth because the blood type of his mother and father were incompatible. He also told me you paid him an extremely large amount of money not to tell Cristo about the blood transfusion."

"Go to hell." Rosario threw her drink in his face.

Enraged, Damien crushed his mouth to hers. But when she struggled against him, she'd miscalculated his strength. His arms tightened, locking around her like two steel bands.

Desperate, she bit down hard on his lips and immediately tasted his blood.

Damien howled and slapped her across the face. Pain exploded across her eyes and through her jaw, sending her onto the floor.

He stepped back and wiped the back of his hand across his mouth. Blood smeared his skin. "I didn't want to play rough tonight. Brutality might turn on men like your husband, but it normally isn't my style. But if you insist—"

"No," Rosario said softly. She hung her head, let the tears come to her eyes. "I'll take care of your needs tonight, Damien."

"That's better," he admonished. His chest puffed up with masculine pleasure. He reached down, grabbed her elbow and helped her to her feet. "I'm glad you see it my way."

"You left me little choice." She stepped back and used a nearby end table for support. "If we're going to do this, at least lock the door like you first suggested. So there are no more interruptions."

"Of course, my dear."

Rosario waited for him to turn away, then she slid the drawer open and pulled out Cristo's small pistol. Surprisingly, her hands weren't shaking.

She thumbed off the safety, praying that there were bullets in the gun.

"I've had a change of heart, Damien." When the captain turned back around, she raised the pistol and pointed it at his chest. "I'm calling this deal off."

Slowly, she squeezed the trigger.

Chapter Twenty

Rosario's scream hit the air. On its heels came another gun-shot. Argus raced out of his father's study and into the sitting room.

A man lay at the foot of the couch. Blood soaked the white linen shirt. The man's dead eyes stared at the ceiling.

"Mama!"

"Stay there!" Rosario ordered when her son came into the room. "I'm okay."

Blood ran down her chin, covered her chest. Whether it was hers or the man's, Argus couldn't be sure.

But she managed, with effort, to straighten. Then slowly she walked to her son. "Argus, your father is going to be furious when he gets here. I had to...stop his business associate. The captain got drunk and attacked me."

"Are you all right?"

"Yes, yes," she said and glanced nervously up at the open doorway. "I have to tell you something quickly. And you have to trust me, *mijo*. I promise I'll explain more to you later. But right now, you just need to listen. And don't ask your questions."

Argus nodded.

"I need you to free Jason Marsh from the cell downstairs."

"The key is gone."

Rosario reached between her breasts and pulled out the

key. "I took them from your father's desk earlier this evening. I was going to set him free myself."

"But how do you know Jason?"

"He was my friend, long before he was yours," she said, then quickly knelt in front of her son. "Listen to me, Argus, and try to understand. Your father is a very powerful man and he desperately wanted a son to rule his empire with. So much that he was going to kill me and find another woman to take my place when I could not get pregnant. I suspected that it was your father who could not have babies, so I decided to get pregnant by another man. To save my life. That man was Jason."

"What are you saying? That Jason is my father?" Emotions tripped through him, confusion, relief, fear…joy. He'd dreamed of this very thing. Of Jason being his father.

"Yes," she replied and gave him a long hug, squeezing almost too hard, but Argus didn't mind. Somehow her arms around him stopped his chest from hurting with fear.

"I don't regret what I did, because God gave me you. But I do regret making you stay here and pretending that a monster like Cristo Delgado was your real father."

She stood then. "I need you to go now. Help Jason out of the cell and then go with him. He will take care of you until I can meet up with you again."

"Come with me, Mama." He tugged on her hand, his voice filled with fear.

"No. I need to keep your father distracted, to give you both time to escape." She kissed his cheek and took another quick hug. "Go. Now."

"But, Mama—"

"Please." Rosario deliberately softened her throbbing lips into some kind of smile. "I love you, *mijo*. It will all be over soon."

"I love you, too."

Argus took one last look at his mother and ran from the room.

Rosario turned toward the captain, her mind already on what she was going to tell her husband.

Suddenly, two hands gripped her neck, forcing all the air from her chest. She clawed at the hands, desperate.

"I heard everything you told your bastard son, Rosario. What do you think I should do about it?" Cristo whispered in her ear as he pulled her back against his chest and tightened his grip. "You think you will go unpunished for your sins, my dear?"

SOLARIS STUDIED THE SCENE before him. The cell had been washed down. Jason Marsh, too. Although the stench still remained, its potency had lessened considerably.

Solaris grudgingly admired the unconscious man on the floor. He'd struggled at first, with a dislocated shoulder and quite a few broken ribs. But Solaris managed to push a tranquilizer down his throat and knocked the operative unconscious.

It was probably a good thing, too. The giant glanced at his watch. He'd been there for several hours, but his mind had not been on catching Argus in the act. Somehow his gut instinct told him that the boy would show up tonight.

Even so, his thoughts had been on Rosario and her dinner with Captain Stravos.

"Jason?"

Solaris straightened from the wall. He heard the soft tap of feet nearby.

When the boy walked past, Solaris simply reached out and grabbed him by the cuff of the neck.

"What are you doing here, Argus?"

"I—"

When the boy didn't respond, Solaris picked him up slightly onto his toes, just to put a little fear in him. "Answer me."

The boy's chin tightened, his mouth flattened into a stubborn line.

"Leave the boy alone, you son of a bitch." The words were raw, slurred, but the threat was there.

Jason moved slowly to the cell bars. Sweat ran in rivets down his face from fighting the drug.

Solaris lessened his grip, but did not let the boy go. "Why don't we end this tonight, Marsh? Tell me where you've hidden the MONGREL."

"Let me out of here and I'll end it," Jason sneered. "Why don't you take on me instead of the boy?"

Jason glanced over at Argus and froze. "You're covered in blood. Are you hurt?"

Argus looked down at his shirt and saw the red splotches. Still shaken, he answered without thought. "It's my mother's. Hers and a friend of my father's, Captain Stravos. He attacked my mother. She shot him with her pistol. He's dead."

"Are you sure?" Solaris demanded.

"Yes," Argus answered, but leaned away from the rage in the giant's face. "She is waiting for my father in the study."

"Damn it, Rosario." Solaris bit out the words under his breath. Suddenly, he dropped Argus to the floor. "Get the hell out of here, boy."

Then Solaris disappeared in three long strides through the passageway.

"Let's go, Argus," Jason urged, holding up his wrists, exposing the shackles. "Do you have the key?"

Startled for a moment, Argus stared at Jason. "Yes. My mother told me to help you, then ask that you keep me safe. She thinks that my father...I mean, that Cristo will try to kill me."

"Cristo?" Jason repeated, suddenly realizing. "Your mom told you, didn't she?"

"That you're my father? Yes," Argus replied softly. He turned the lock and opened the door. "But we must help my mother, Jason."

"We will, I promise," Jason answered. The boy unlocked the shackles and let them drop to the ground. Jason rubbed his wrists to get the circulation back. "Where is Julia, Argus?"

"I don't know. I left her with Calvin at the cemetery. I think he knows I am your son, Jason."

Jason swore. "Okay. First, I'm going to get you out of here. Then I'll come back for your mother. She would want it that way."

"I'm not going without her." The boy's chin stuck out, determined. "You promised."

Jason took a step, his legs trembled. He locked his knees and grabbed for the concrete wall.

"And you cannot do this without me," Argus argued.

"Then I guess it's a good thing I'm here," Cal said from behind them.

Chapter Twenty-One

Cal placed Jason's good arm around his shoulders.

Julia grabbed Argus. "Are you okay, sweetheart?"

"Yes, but my mama—"

"We heard," Cal said. "Like…your father told you though, we need to get you safe first. Julia will stay with you while we go back for your mother."

"Solaris is already on his way," Jason said.

They met very little resistance going back out of the villa. Most of the men were out searching for them across the grounds and outside the compound.

Within moments, they reached the edge of the courtyard where the shadows masked their presence.

"What now?"

"Back through the cemetery," Cal stated. "Right?"

"Yes," Argus said. "By the crypt."

"All right, but we move fast."

Suddenly, floodlights shattered the darkness, blinding the group.

Julia automatically hugged Argus to her side.

"You're not going anywhere, I think." Cristo stepped out from behind them. "I've waited a long time for this."

Cal felt a sharp jab in his spine. "Drop the gun, West," Solaris said, his voice a mere rasp of air.

Cal tossed the gun to the ground.

"That was a quick change of plans," Jason sneered.

"Shut up." Jorgie shoved him to the ground, kicked him in the stomach, doubling Jason over into a fetal position. But Cal noticed Jason did not cry out in pain. He didn't give Jorgie the satisfaction.

"Not quick enough for Rosario it seems." Solaris kicked Cal's pistol out of reach of both men.

Julia heard the underlying derision in the giant's tone and immediately understood.

Rosario was dead.

Argus stiffened beside Julia. He, too, understood. "My mother?"

"Dead," Cristo said with no inflection in his voice.

"Cal," Julia warned quietly, but her gaze slid past Cal to just beyond the lights.

Cal saw dozens of silhouettes outlined, each holding rifles, others machine guns. Most were pointed at him and Jason.

"Looks like I've finally got your attention," Cristo said loud and sharp. When neither man responded, Cristo nodded to Jorgie.

"I haven't seen you since the airport." Jorgie strolled over to Cal. "Miss me?"

Jorgie drove his fist into Cal's stomach. He doubled over and dropped to his knees.

"Not as much as you missed me, obviously." Cal coughed up the bile that slapped at the back of his throat.

Jorgie took his machine gun and slammed it into Cal's back. Pain exploded, nearly rupturing Cal's spine. He struggled to breathe through it.

"Now we're even." Jorgie laughed.

"Ms. Cutting." Cristo greeted her as if they were at a dinner party. "I'm glad you could join us. I've been looking forward to meeting you for some time."

He strolled over until he was standing directly in front of

her. Suddenly, he gripped her throat just beneath her jaw and squeezed.

Julia sensed Cal go deadly still behind her.

"We are going to have quite the conversation later," he murmured. "I hope you're looking forward to it as much as I am."

Julia glared at him, but said nothing—afraid that any confrontation would push Calvin to do something foolish to protect her.

"Solaris, bring Marsh to me."

Solaris grabbed Jason by the hair and dragged him over to Cristo's feet.

"Are we done playing games, Mr. Marsh?"

Cristo pointed his pistol at the agent. "Are you going to tell me where the MONGREL prototype is?"

"He doesn't know," Cal interjected.

"Shut up, West," Jason rasped, then glared at Cristo. Blood glistened, flowing from the cut on Jason's face down his chin. Giving him the look of a madman. "Go ahead, you son of a bitch. Pull the trigger."

Jorgie kicked Jason in the back of the head, sending him sprawling.

Argus stepped forward, then hesitated. "Don't," Julia warned, then grabbed the boy and pulled him back.

"It's amazing how fast you've changed loyalties, *son.*"

Argus stared at Jason, who lay still on the ground, unconscious.

"I don't care about him," he said to Cristo. Tears wet his cheeks. But his hands clenched and unclenched at his sides.

"But do they care about you?" Cristo asked Argus before his eyes scanned the three adults. "By the end of the day, we will know for sure, now won't we?"

"It's time for you to make a choice, West." Suddenly, the drug lord pointed the gun at Argus. "So what will it be? The child? Your friend?" He swung the gun barrel toward Julia. "Your lover?"

He cocked the hammer with his thumb. "Or the several thousand poor, little rich kids who get their kicks off my cocaine?"

"WHY NOT ME FIRST, CRISTO?" Cal suggested. "That's what you've wanted for a while, anyway. This…" His hand waved around the courtyard. "This was never about gaining control of the MONGREL, was it? It's all about this moment and your vendetta against Jason and myself. Tell me, Cristo, what bothers you more? The fact that I was the one who got away? The one man who almost killed you. The one who threatened your inner sanctum? The great Delgado family?"

Cristo laughed, a harsh sound that grated deep in his throat. "Haven't you heard? I have no family anymore. Even my daughter has turned against me. The girl actually thinks she can sue me for custody of the boy." Cristo spat on the ground. "It does not matter now, does it? He'll die with the rest of you."

"You might not have a family, but you still hide behind your men."

"I *lead* my men, West."

"Even when you're not quite a man yourself?" Cal continued taunting. "Everyone knows now that Jason gave Rosario what you couldn't manage yourself. A son."

"She was a whore." Cristo cursed and took a step forward. "Now she isn't even that."

"Deep down you knew Argus couldn't be yours. How many women have you slept with in your lifetime and have gotten pregnant? Not one, I'm sure. You were lucky to have your daughter. If she really is your daughter. It wasn't your wives who couldn't have kids, it was you. Not quite the man you wanted to be remembered as, are you?"

"Man? You speak of men when you're nothing more than a British pig." Cristo shoved his pistol at Solaris. "I'll kill you with my bare hands."

"Come get me, you bastard," Jason rasped from the ground.

"Remember Argus, Jason," Julia warned softly. She tightened her arm around the boy and drew him to her side.

"Yes, Marsh. Remember your son," Cristo mocked, glancing over at Argus.

The boy lifted his chin, ignored the tears on his cheeks and stepped away from Julia.

Cristo spoke directly to Argus. "After I kill West, I will take care of the woman and your father while you watch, boy. Then you and I will have a painful talk about loyalties."

"That's so courageous of you, Cristo. Threatening to torture a boy," Cal snorted, deliberately drawing Cristo's attention back. "You're not a man, Cristo. You're a coward. And I promise I'll bury you before we're done."

"And I promise to bury you alive," Cristo bellowed, his hands fisted and up.

Cal shifted into a predatory stance.

"Put all the lights down here," Cristo ordered.

Almost instantly, a circle of spotlights hit Cal. Momentarily blinded, Cristo tackled him, slammed him back into the dirt.

The guards cheered their leader. Others fired rifles into the air.

"Hear that, West? My men are loyal. I am respected!"

Cal's back slammed into the ground, jarring his body. Cristo scrambled to his feet. Cal rolled over just as Cristo's foot came down toward his head.

"They cheer because they are too stupid to know better." Cal rolled again and came up on his feet. "Is this how it was with Esteban, Cristo? You had your men do your dirty work?"

"Esteban is done," Cristo spat. "Why do you think this shipment is so important? Why the device is more important?"

"You finally think you found a way to put him out of business, is that it?"

"More than put him out of business," Cristo corrected, his breath coming in heavy gasps. "Destroy him."

"Jealous of his success?" Cal circled the drug lord. "Or finally realized the extent of your inadequacy?"

Cristo roared, a bull enraged. He charged, but this time Cal was ready. He stepped to the side, brought up his knee, caught Cristo in the face, shattering his nose.

One of the guards stepped forward, raised his rifle. A shot rang out and the man dropped his weapon. A small bullet hole marked dead center of his forehead. The man fell forward, lifeless.

"You son of a bitch," Jorgie screamed and stepped forward.

Solaris kept his rifle raised and pointed at the other man's chest. "Twitch and I will kill you."

Slowly, Jorgie dropped his machine gun to the ground and moved his hands to his sides. But anger blotched his pock-marked cheeks.

Solaris told Calvin, "Finish this."

Cristo swore, realizing for the first time that Solaris was backing Calvin. "You son of a bitch," he said, then spat blood on the ground. "I'll see you dead."

Cal took the opening and let go with a round kick that caught Cristo in the jaw. The drug lord staggered back, his knees buckled, his hand found Jorgie's rifle. He pointed the barrel toward Calvin.

Without warning, a gunshot hit the air. Cristo grunted, then looked down. Blood spread across his chest.

"I killed you first, Papa," Argus shouted, tears streaming down his cheeks.

Cristo fell backward onto the ground, his body trembling, his chest heaving.

Slowly, Argus walked over to Jason and dropped the pistol in front of him. "You promised to save my mother. And I believed you."

"Argus—" Jason started.

But the boy shook his head and walked over to Julia.

Jason picked up the pistol. Julia immediately recognized the pearl handle. "Where did you get the gun, Argus?"

"From Padre Dominic's room."

She hugged the boy tight to her chest.

Solaris walked over to Cristo. The drug lord groaned and looked at the giant.

"Julia, cover the boy's eyes," Cal said quietly.

Solaris pointed the gun and fired point-blank into Cristo's forehead. "For Rosario."

He glanced at the boy. "You did what needed to be done. Never regret your actions."

A roar of rage hit the air. Without warning, Jorgie dropped to his knees and rolled, coming up crouched with his assault rifle in his hands.

"Get down!" Cal screamed as Jorgie's weapon swung toward Argus and Julia.

Cal dove into the South American. The assault rifle discharged. Cal felt the punch in his stomach, his side catch on fire.

Through the pain, his hand found the other man's knife.

Jorgie grunted with pleasure, his eyes on Cal's. "I killed you, West."

Cal shoved the knife up under Jorgie's ribs. Realization etched the other man's features. His body went lax. Cal used the last of his strength to shove Jorgie away.

The man slumped to the ground. Dead before he hit the dirt.

Cal's knees buckled. He tried to keep upright, but the ground tilted beneath his feet.

"Cal!" Through the haze of pain, he felt Julia beside him. She gripped his arm and eased him to the ground.

"Couldn't...let...him...shoot...you...the boy." Fire burned in his chest, stopping the words.

Tears ran down Julia's cheeks. "Stay with me, Cal! I mean it! If you don't, I won't tell you where I hid the MONGREL. I mean it! I won't tell anyone."

"In...the...bear."

Chapter Twenty-Two

Grainger's Bar was located on the edge of D.C.'s Georgetown district. A tribute to the owner's sense of humor.

An English bar right near the Yank's Naval Academy.

The owner, Michael Grainger—a retired British naval officer—served with his father through two wars. And several police actions.

The neighborhood bar had been there for years. A place that Cal frequented many times as a young boy with his father. The first place Cal ever got drunk.

And right now, he certainly needed to get drunk.

A shot glass slammed on the table rousing Cal from his thoughts. "You still here?"

"Yep," Jason said. "We need to talk. But I can wait until you're ready."

Grainger walked up to the men in the booth. He set a fifth of scotch on the table between them. "Now, you chaps best behave this time. I don't want to come back to find my place the mess you left it last time."

"I didn't do anything," Cal argued, his head pounding from lack of painkillers. "My friend here got too enthusiastic over making a point."

"I left cash on the bar for the damage."

"And it took three weeks to get it taken care of," Grainger countered. "My customers suffered."

"No fights tonight," Jason promised. "Just a few drinks."

"All right then," Grainger said, then patted Cal on the shoulder. "Tell your father I said hello, Cal. I'm closing up. The taxicab number is written on the bottle label. Make sure you lock the door on the way out."

The big man whistled in a soft, off-tune melody as he walked away.

"If you don't go away, Marsh, I just might shoot you again."

Jason considered the possibility for almost half a minute. "Might let you. Seemed to work out for me last time."

"What the hell are you talking about?"

"After you put a bullet in my leg, it ended up getting infected. Took me weeks to recover."

"So?"

"I recovered at Delgado's villa," Jason continued. "Under the special care of Rosario."

"That's when you got her pregnant."

Jason studied the shot of whiskey for a moment, then downed the whole thing. "I can honestly say she seduced me, mate. Didn't find out until much later."

"So why aren't you with your newfound family?"

"I'm working on it," Jason replied without taking offense. "I could ask you the same question."

"No questions. Just say what you have to, Marsh, and then get the bloody hell out of my life."

"You called me for a ride home from the hospital, remember," Jason remarked, his brows drawn together.

"Only because Cain left orders with the hospital not to call me a taxi. Bloody military hospitals. You were the only one I knew who didn't give a damn that I checked out a few days early."

"Almost a week early. Considering you just had major stomach surgery, most people would be worried," Jason commented, then tapped the whiskey bottle. "I'd have to agree. As much as I like the idea of you suffering, this is a bit much. Isn't it?"

Cal slammed back his shot. "If you're staying here just to babysit—"

"Actually, I'm here to knock some sense into your head." Jason poured Cal and himself another two fingers. "You're a mess, West. You must be in love."

Cal swore, telling Jason exactly what he thought of his opinion. He laid his head back against the booth and closed his eyes, hoping Marsh might take the hint.

"She's leaving," Jason stated.

"It'll be better for her. She's not cut out for this town."

Jason snorted. "You know as well as I do that she could run this town and the people in it. I think that's one of the things that used to scare me about her."

Cal raised his head, opened his eyes and cocked an eyebrow, then immediately regretted it when a sharp pain shot through his forehead.

"Look, here's the deal. She loves you and it's the right kind of love. Not the kind you and I are used to. What she's giving you is a gift and you're walking away from it."

"It's not her that's the problem, Marsh. It's me. She deserves a better life than sharing mine."

"Bugger that," Jason retorted. "Then give her that life, you stupid son of a bitch. Share hers."

"I'm an unemployed government assassin. That won't go very far on my résumé," Cal stated.

"You've got money—"

"It's not enough," Cal snapped.

"Then use some of it to buy you time to decide," Jason said.

They heard the front door slam shut.

"Go away, we're closed," Cal yelled, disgusted. All he

wanted was some peace and to get slowly drunk out of his mind on whiskey.

"That's my cue." Jason got up, reached into his pocket and pulled out some cash. He threw it on the table.

"What the hell does that mean?"

"It means, I'm your ride, Cal." Julia walked up to the booth.

"I called her," Jason said and gave Cal a short salute. "I'm off to mess up my own life some more. You're going to have to figure yours out on your own, West."

He leaned over and gave Julia a kiss on the cheek. "Be kind to him, he's slow."

Julia nodded, then grabbed his arm as he walked away. "Please be careful, Jason."

Cal scowled but said nothing.

Jason patted her hand. "I will."

After he left, Julia reached for the scotch and poured herself two fingers. She picked up the glass. "Cheers, Cal."

She slammed the drink back in one gulp.

When she reached for the bottle again, he snatched it from the table. "What the bloody hell are you doing?"

"Something I should have done a long time ago," she admitted. Without waiting for an answer, she got up and walked over to the bar. "There's bound to be more, right?"

She slipped behind the counter and searched the shelves. A moment later, she came back with another bottle of MacAlister whiskey. She clinked her bottle against the one Cal held. "His and hers. Beats bathroom towels."

She poured the whiskey until it hit the brim of the shot glass. "You see, for the first time in my life, I'm not hindered by rules and social etiquette. Growing up, my marriage to Jason, even working for Jon Mercer, I had no choice but to be politically correct, follow social graces."

She swallowed part of the shot, then blinked when it hit the back of her throat.

"Now, I'm not the Goody Two-shoes of Capitol Hill anymore. I quit my job and am currently unemployed. And free to do as I please."

If she wanted to drink herself sick, it was fine with him. He'd call the taxi for both of them.

"Why did you tell Jason to be careful?"

"He's flying to New York," Julia replied. "It seems Alejandra Delgado went to court and has been granted custody of Argus. She claimed Jason was an unfit parent. The New York court system agreed."

"Jason's going to fight for Argus?"

"It looks that way," Julia answered. "He quit the DEA. He's going back into law."

"That's going to be interesting," Cal commented. "I almost wish I could watch."

"I can think of a lot of other words besides interesting."

"Such as?"

"Ugly," she answered. "Jason's changed, but I'm not sure for the better. He's directed all of his rage at Alejandra. I hope she can handle it."

"And the boy?" Cal asked. "What does he want?"

"I'm not sure," she answered. "But I know what he needs is stability and love. I'm not so sure Jason's ready to give him that yet."

Rather than her usual tailored business suit, she wore a black leather jacket that skimmed the waist of her slim-fitting black jeans, the curve of her hips. Underneath the jacket was an oversize cowl-neck sweater of deep bronze that set off the gold highlights of her hair and matched the suede brown boots that stopped just below her knees.

"So all the changes you've made since we returned from South America—the hair, the clothes, the whiskey," he observed when she downed another shot. "What is this all about, Julia?"

"Oh, no, you don't, Cal, not yet," she ordered. "It's my turn to ask the questions. But I want the truth."

Her skin flushed pink—from the whiskey or her temper, he couldn't be sure.

"But will you trust the answers?"

"Yes."

He sat back and studied her. "Okay, then I'll answer truthfully."

"Not so fast." She stood, giving herself room to move around.

"Calvin Francis West. Do you swear to tell the whole truth and nothing but the truth so help you God?"

Cal quirked an eyebrow at her. "You're serious."

"Answer the question," she stated. A lawyer's voice, cool and collected. And sexy as hell.

Cal felt a stir in the deepest part of his gut. Bloody hell, it was actually making him hard.

"I do."

She nodded, satisfied, then placed both her hands on the table and leaned forward. A piece of hair fell over her eye; she blew it out of the way. "Tell this court. For the last several years, you have worked for various governments. What was your main purpose?"

"Main purpose?"

"I believe the term is specialty. What was your specialty?"

"Killing."

Julia straightened, caught off guard at the directness of his answer.

"Are you still employed by said governments?"

"No," Cal answered. He folded his hands on the table. It was either that or pull her onto his lap. "I resigned my position with Labyrinth a few days ago."

She nodded, then turned away. A moment later, she faced him, her back rigid, her features carefully blank. "Have you killed anyone who didn't deserve it?"

"No," Cal answered. "I specialized in jungle warfare. Ninety percent of my kills were drug or arms related."

"And the other ten percent?"

"Self-defense."

"I see," she acknowledged with a curt nod. "Were you sent in originally, not only to kidnap Argus, but to kill him?"

"What?" Cal swore. "I don't kill children, Julia. And Cain and Jon would never have asked me to."

"And Jason? Would you have killed him?"

"If he'd been proven a traitor, I would have neutralized him if necessary."

"And Renalto," she asked almost as an afterthought. "Did you or did you not know that he was a possible traitor to the United States government?"

"I talked with Renalto and Esteban the morning before we went to the airstrip while you were sleeping. That's why I was certain Esteban was taking you with him. He'd already told me," Cal explained. "Renalto told me he was undercover trying to oust the mole in D.C. feeding Delgado information on our operations."

"Cain told me it was Ernest Becenti," she commented, then flashed back over those few days. "That's why you left Renalto behind at the airstrip. Isn't it?"

"Yes," Cal replied. "Once Delgado attacked, I knew Renalto couldn't be seen leaving with us. Jorgie or Solaris would have seen him. It would have blown his cover. He was too close to finding out about Becenti."

"And Esteban? You were expecting him to show up at the compound, too?"

"They showed up late, but yes I was expecting them," Cal

said derisively. "Would have saved myself some pain if they had showed up on time."

"You trusted Esteban. Why?"

"I trusted his motivation, more than I trusted the man," Cal corrected. "As much as protecting you might have put him in good with President Mercer, he gave himself a better advantage by using his men to take over Delgado's compound. Saving Labyrinth's best operatives, the President's secretary and delivering the MONGREL would make him and Jon Mercer practically family. That's one hell of a motivation for him to stay on the straight and narrow."

She nodded, then changed the subject, needing to process her emotions over his answers. "Renalto says hello, by the way."

Cal lifted an eyebrow, but didn't object to the change. "I heard he earned some time off. Cain said he's taking an extended vacation somewhere."

Julia smiled, a big grin that made his heart leap. "Hollywood, for starters. He's going to spend a few months there then head to France for the Cannes Film Festival."

"You're joking." Cal laughed. A full laugh, deep in the back of his throat, the core of his chest. Goose bumps tripped over her skin. She gasped in surprise.

"What's the matter, Julia?"

"You're laughing." Stunned, she could only gawk at Cal. His whole face changed. The boyish features broke through the hard lines, taking her breath away. "I've never heard you laugh, Cal."

"I never heard you question a witness," Cal answered, his voice dropped and grew husky. "I think I'm going to want to hear it more often."

"You just might," Julia said, her body reacting to the searing look, the tone of his words. "Jason's not the only one thinking about practicing law again."

"You can practice with me some more," Cal said easily, but the tone was deceptive, deep.

The hair stood up on the back of Julia's neck.

Suddenly, losing her footing, she glanced around. "Is it getting hot in here?" She blew out a burst of air.

"Could be," Cal said. He poured her another shot. "Drink this, it might help."

She laughed at the lecherous look in his face. "I think I'll just remove my jacket."

Cal watched as she slipped it off her shoulders. "That works, too," he observed. "Feel free to shed as much as you want."

She winked at him, slow and sexy. "I will."

Blood raced from Cal's head and pooled in his lap. He shifted to get a little more comfortable in his jeans.

"I have a question, Jules."

Julia froze. Cal hadn't used his nickname for her the whole time they'd been together. "Go ahead."

"Why didn't you come to see me at the hospital?"

"I really wanted to, Cal," Julia answered, her heart in her eyes. "But I didn't think my being there would help with your recovery."

"And if you realized I had wanted you there?" he asked softly, but she knew everything hinged on this question.

"I would have moved in and slept every night beside you."

He grunted, but she also sensed the relief that went through him.

"I think if you had, I would have had a much faster recovery." Suddenly, he pulled her into his lap. His arousal was hard underneath her thigh. "Don't you?"

"Yes," she managed, but it was difficult with his teeth nibbling on her ear. "Are we good, Cal?"

"Any more questions?"

"One," she replied.

"The bear?"

"All right. Two questions." She smiled. "How *did* you know I hid the MONGREL in the teddy bear?"

"I figured out it was a possibility on the plane and I replayed the conversation we had in the apartment through my head," Cal said. "But I didn't believe it at first. It took until I realized you trusted me to save Argus, not hurt him. Then I realized you trusted me with the device also. Right?"

"So why didn't you tell Cain?" she asked.

"Simple. I wanted to see it for myself," Cal said. "I needed to see the hard evidence that you did trust me with doing the right thing."

"But Cain confiscated it immediately after we hit the States," Julia said. "How did—"

"Regina made Cain bring it to the hospital." Cal laughed against her neck, making her skin tingle, her pulse leap. "He opened the bear at the foot of my bed."

"It wasn't a conscious thought, you know," Julia admitted. "In fact, I didn't realize my motive behind it until you were shot saving me and Argus."

"And the second question, Counselor?"

"Do you love me as much as I love you, Calvin West?"

"More," he murmured against her lips. "So much more than I ever thought possible."

* * * * *